THE UNLUCKY BRIDE RESCUE

TEXAS HOTLINE SERIES, BOOK #11

JO GRAFFORD

Second Edition. This book was previously part of the Disaster City Search and Rescue Series. It has since been revised and recovered to be included in the Texas Hotline Series.

Cover Design by Jo Grafford

ISBN: 978-1-63907-034-3

ACKNOWLEDGMENTS

I'm so grateful to my editor, Cathleen Weaver, and to my amazing beta readers — Mahasani, Debbie Turner, and Pigchevy. I also want to give a shout-out to my Cuppa Jo Readers on Facebook for reading and loving my books!

GET A FREE BOOK!

Join my mailing list to be the first to know about new releases, free books, special discount prices, Bonus Content, and giveaways.

https://BookHip.com/JNNHTK

ABOUT THIS SERIES

Welcome to the Texas Hotline, a team of search and rescue experts — police officers, firefighters, expert divers, and more. In an emergency, your sweet and swoon-worthy rescuer is only a phone call away.

CHAPTER 1: SEPARATION AGREEMENT

SEVEN

Please don't go. Seven Colburn's heart felt like it was going to crack in two as his wife picked up her pair of black vinyl suitcases and moved toward the front door of their apartment. He would've gotten on his knees and begged her to stay if he thought it would do a bit of good. But it wouldn't.

Her mind was made up. She was leaving him.

Their dog, Goliath, gave a bark of protest. As if sensing that something was wrong, the enormous black Doberman Pinscher trotted after her.

"No, Goliath." Tiffany Colburn's voice broke as she shook her head at him. "Stay!" she commanded softly. She cleared her throat before speaking again, this time to Seven. "I left a copy of our separation agreement on the bar in the kitchen." Her face was averted, her voice low and strained.

"Don't know why you're calling it that," he

growled. "I sure as heck didn't agree to anything." The only reason he'd signed the stupid paperwork was because she'd insisted it was either that or a divorce.

"Please don't make this any harder than it already is," she sighed.

"Tiff." He tossed his Stetson on the couch in the living room and followed after her. "I would do anything to change your mind. You know that. Anything you ask," he added wearily. It had been an exhausting week of duty with the Texas Rangers, leaving him in no condition to argue with her again this evening. He was dead on his feet.

"This has been a long time coming, Seven. I'm not changing my mind." She reached the door and set one of her suitcases down to reach for the door handle.

Even from this angle, with her back to him and her whole body tense, she was beautiful. Unfortunately, he'd never been very good with words. He hadn't told her often enough how lovely, intelligent, and talented she was; how hilarious at times and how heartwarming at other times. Most importantly, he hadn't stressed enough how vital she was to his happiness.

Out of sheer habit, he jogged across the room to reach around her to open the door for her. She was wearing a pair of black yoga pants beneath one of her favorite oversized sweatshirts. Pink, this time. The whole time they'd been together, she'd worn her shirts a size or two bigger than necessary, claiming it hid the extra fifteen or twenty pounds she swore she could never get rid of. He'd never found any fault with her weight or size and had no idea what she was so worried about. He loved her just the way she was. In hindsight, that was something else they probably should have talked about more.

With a sharp intake of breath, his wife retrieved her suitcase and stepped across the threshold into the sultry June breeze.

"At least tell me where you're going," he pleaded. The sun was setting, and it would be getting dark soon. The rowdiest element of Houston would be hitting the streets of the downtown district soon. She hadn't made it out of his sight yet, and he was already frantic with worry on behalf of the blonde, curvy woman who'd turned his life upside down.

She paused without turning around. "I'll be staying with my mother tonight," she informed him in a stiff voice.

Of course you are. For reasons he'd never understood, his mother-in-law had always hated him. "And after tonight?" He propped a hand on the door frame.

"I have a job interview in the Dallas area."

Could you be more specific? "You mean tomorrow?" The lawman in him was itching for details.

"You're doing it again." She started to walk again.

"I'm not one of your suspects, and this is the hallway outside our apartment, not some interrogation room."

Okay. Fine! You don't have to bite my head off. "I'm just trying to have a conversation here." He ran a hand through his hair, knowing it had been too long since they had done more than leave notes for each other about why one of them was going to be gone for the evening and which leftovers were up for grabs in the fridge. He hated the way they'd stopped making an effort to meet up over dinner. For the past several months, it had almost felt like they were two strangers living together — both of them coming and going at odd hours and mumbling quick greetings as they passed each other in the hallway. It was no wonder she wanted out of the shambles their marriage had become.

"My interview is taking place soon," she announced vaguely. "I'll let you know if I end up taking the job. Until then, I need you to give me some space, Seven." She finally glanced over her shoulder to fix her baby blues on him in a bleak look of warning. "I mean it." Her features were pale but resolute.

Her message was clear. *Don't call.*

He recognized the expression all too well. It meant his wife had truly made up her mind. She could be pretty stubborn sometimes. They both could.

When she got like this, though, it never failed to

spark his anger. It wasn't that he couldn't handle a marital spat. Lord knew they'd enjoyed their fair share of them in recent months, but how could she just throw in the towel and walk out on him? On them? On their entire marriage? It felt off somehow, completely out of character for her. Unless he was losing his mind, he could've sworn she'd enjoyed the making-up part after their fights every bit as much as he did.

"So that's it?" He slapped his hands against the door frame in a burst of bitterness. "You're just quitting on us?"

"Don't try to put this all on me," she snapped. "You checked out on our marriage a long time ago." She reached the stairs and paused again.

Knowing how her mind worked, he figured she was mentally rehearsing whatever final goodbye speech she'd prepared. He had no interest in hearing it. He already knew that she was tired of his long work hours. He understood that she was terrified about losing him to the many dangers he faced at his job every day. He also understood that there were things he was going to have to change soon, especially once they were ready to start a family.

Since she'd made those things clear during past arguments, he skipped forward to the bottom line. "I love you, Tiff." His tone was quiet and resolute. "I haven't said it as often as you deserve to hear it, because apparently I'm an idiot. But the fact that you married an idiot in no way changes the fact that you're the most beautiful person I know — inside and out."

Her face paled, but she didn't look near ready to kiss and make up.

Feeling less sure of where they stood with each other more than ever before, he mumbled, "I guess what I'm trying to say is, I really hope you find what you're looking for out there." He waved tiredly at the door. If she really wanted to go, he couldn't stop her. "And I hope it brings you home to me."

Though her back was to him, her shoulders started to shake. She mumbled something that sounded like, "Please don't do this." Then she hurried down the stairs, weeping in whispery gasps. It was as if she was trying to cry in silence but wasn't quite able to pull it off.

Goliath leaped up from the corner of the living room, where she'd instructed him to park himself on his haunches. He joined Seven in the doorway, barking frenziedly.

Every instinct in Seven told him to run after his wife, but he knew it wasn't what she wanted from him. Not tonight. She'd made it brutally clear that she needed her distance from him.

He stared after her through narrowed lids, wondering what in the world was going on with her this time. Tiff had her quirky moments. Everybody did. He also suspected she had a few secrets from her past that she'd never gotten around to sharing with him. Again, who didn't? But nothing about the legal separation she'd filed for felt right. Or the way she was skedaddling from their apartment like it was on fire.

With a heavy heart, he watched her go, staring at the black iron stairs even when he could no longer see her. He continued to stand in the open doorway when he heard the three tries it took her to get the motor of her old Mercedes coupe started. It was a hand-me-down from her mother, one he'd been meaning to tinker with to see if he could fix the ignition. However, it seemed he'd waited too long for that, too.

Standing there and listening to her ignition glitch out felt like the final straw. Unable to take anymore, he swung around to head back inside the apartment they'd shared for a little over a year. He kicked the door shut behind him while wave after wave of rage and helplessness crashed over him.

Running a hand over his face, he snarled into the empty room, "I should've fixed the ignition." He raised his voice and bellowed in a louder voice. "I should've fixed the blasted ignition!" Just add it to his long list of failures as a husband.

Goliath ran in a semi-circle in front of him, barking.

Though Seven could tell the dog was upset, he didn't know what to say or do to comfort him. On some level, it was strangely comforting to know that the Doberman understood something was wrong. Dogs had pretty amazing instincts like that.

Seven felt like dropping to the floor and howling alongside his dog. Gazing around their small living room, he couldn't help noting how dull the place looked in Tiff's absence. Without her, it was just a room with a threadbare brown suede sofa and the scratched up television stand they'd rescued from the gated-off dumpster area outside shortly after they'd moved in. They had plans to buy a house with real furniture someday, but every penny they'd earned during their first year of marriage had been spent on her college tuition. She'd graduated a week ago with her Associates Degree in Culinary Arts, but they hadn't yet gotten around to celebrating her achievement. They'd been waiting for the next time they managed to take a day off from work together.

Seven realized now that they shouldn't have waited. He should have at least purchased her a card and flowers and maybe ordered take-out from her favorite restaurant. *What was I thinking?* He paced the tiny living room, recalling how difficult it was for either of them to take off work right now. The last time they'd succeeding in doing so on the same day was a little over a year ago. It was the day they'd married — Friday, the thirteenth of May — an unlucky day, according to her mother.

Though he didn't believe in that stuff, it was kind

of hard to argue that their marriage was in real trouble. He stomped back to the kitchen to snatch up the separation agreement from the bar. He'd not yet read it in its entirety. Unlike Tiff, he hadn't even bothered to hire a lawyer. What was the point? They had almost no money or assets to speak of, certainly not enough to fight over. He'd simply signed where she'd asked him to sign. Maybe he was a fool for still trusting her, but he did. Implicitly.

His gaze fell on the pink note she'd stuck to the top of the legal agreement. It read:

Withdrew $5,000 from our savings account today. I'll send you back your half as soon as I can. —T

It was more bad news. *Aw, man, Tiff! Really?* Seven stared at her note, knowing it meant yet another one of his dreams was about to be flushed down the toilet. He'd been counting on their pitifully small savings to cover his tuition at the Texas Hotline Training Center next month. Since his wife was currently between jobs, he doubted she'd have the money paid back that soon.

As bad as the timing was for her to empty out their savings account, it was his fault for not telling her he had the money earmarked for something else. Unfortunately, his admission to the renowned training program was yet another item they'd never gotten around to talking out. If they had, Tiff wouldn't have touched the money. He was sure of it.

However, with their marriage on the rocks, it hadn't seemed prudent to mention to her that he was planning on being absent from home for an entire month. *Well, not any longer.*

He tossed the separation agreement back on the bar, knowing there was no way he could afford it now. He'd call the training center in the morning to cancel the slot they'd offered him. He'd already delayed his start date once. He doubted they'd be willing to postpone it a second time.

The only reason he'd applied to the training center was to position himself for a career change, maybe as a training subcontractor in the law enforcement community. For Tiff's sake, he'd been planning on taking whatever opportunity presented itself first that led to better hours and better pay. That was the kind of stuff a guy did for a wife who wanted a family. Without a wife, though, there'd be no family. And without a family, it no longer mattered what kind of hours he worked.

His cell phone buzzed with an incoming call that he was in no mood to answer. He didn't even bother taking it out of his pocket. When it buzzed a second time, he ignored it again. The third time it started buzzing, however, he lifted it to his ear without looking at his Caller ID and growled, "What?"

"There you are," his grandfather chortled. "Figured if I harassed you long enough, you'd eventually pick up."

"This is not a good time, Pops." Seven didn't have the heart to tell the crippled old fellow that Tiff was gone. Skip Colburn worshipped the ground his granddaughter-in-law walked on. This was going to hit him pretty hard. Just not tonight.

"When is it ever?" His grandfather's voice sobered. "Listen, I know about the trouble you and Tiffany are having. I've stayed out of it as best I could, but I reckon there's no need for us to dance around it any longer."

You're kidding! Seven closed his eyes and pinched the bridge of his nose. "How?" The fact that his only living relative was aware of his failed marriage did not make him feel any better about it.

"She told me, son." His grandfather made a sound, as if wanting to say more, then stopped.

"You two talk?" Seven couldn't have been more taken aback. Since when?

"You two don't?" his grandfather returned dryly.

Ouch! That was a low blow. The air seeped out of Seven. "I don't know what to say." He wanted to go find a dark hole somewhere, climb inside it, and start throwing dirt over himself.

"Well, I do have a few things to say about it, if I may." His grandfather's normally matter-of-fact tone held an unexpected thread of empathy.

Seven lowered his forearms to the kitchen bar and leaned on them. "By all means, let me have it."

He braced himself for one of the fellow's classic brow-beatings.

It didn't come.

"I've got venison steaks on the grill out back and was getting ready to start peeling some taters. How long will it take you to get here?"

Seven straightened and glanced at his watch, fearing his grandfather was taking his breakup with Tiff worse than he was letting on. "Twenty minutes if I don't get called in for an emergency."

"I'll see you then." In true Skip Colburn style, he disconnected the line without saying goodbye.

Seven lowered the phone to stare at it for a moment. Then he snorted and jammed it back in his pocket. *Ah, what the heck?* There was no point in delaying the inevitable. If his grandfather needed to vent his spleen about all the mistakes Seven had made in his miserably short marriage, he might as well drive to his place tonight and get it over with. Skip Colburn's wrath wasn't the kind that could be slept off or dulled with time. He said what he meant, and meant what he said.

Whatever he had to say, though, he planned to do it over venison steaks. At least Seven would get a free meal out of it.

"Come on, Goliath." He snapped his fingers at the dog to indicate it was time to go. Leaving him in the apartment would simply earn him another warning note from management about the dog's incessant barking. Besides, they could skip their evening run if Goliath worked off enough steam at the farm.

Retrieving his Stetson, Seven left the apartment, wallowing in misery and trying not to think about how heavy Tiff's suitcases had been when she'd lugged them down the stairs only minutes earlier. He also tried not to look at the spot where she liked to park, beneath a scraggly Honeylocust that she swore kept her car from heating up too much on the hottest days. Her choice of parking spots had also kept her windshield spattered with bird poo, since the black-birds enjoyed roosting in the branches of the tree above her car.

Yeah, I'm staring at your parking spot even though I told myself I wouldn't. Seven felt like his limbs were weighed down by lead as he opened the door of his rusty black Ford pickup. He whistled for Goliath to climb in. The dog leaped through the door and settled on the passenger side of the seat, wiggling in anticipation of the drive ahead.

Though he'd originally been trained by a volunteer team as a search and rescue dog, his handler had been pretty laid back. As a result, the dog didn't possess the rigid discipline of a police dog. It was something Seven had been planning on fixing during his spare time. However, spare time was something he had precious little of these days.

Gripping the steering wheel, Seven gave Tiff's

empty parking spot one last hard glance before starting the ignition. *Tiff, what am I going to do without you?* She smiled back at him from the small picture of her he had clipped to his sun visor. Her beautiful smile was still the screen saver on his phone, and he carried a picture of her in his wallet, too. Yeah, he had it that bad for her.

Even while their marriage was struggling during the past several months, she was the brightest part of his existence. After spending his pre-teen years in foster care and most of his high school years beneath the tutelage of a retired Texas Ranger, he wasn't exactly the product of motherly nurturing. Tiffany was the only woman who'd ever dared to take him and his issues on full-time. She'd endured his inner scars, outer rough edges, and overall lack of polish. Well, right up to the point where she'd stopped.

Unable to bear the sound of his own thoughts any longer, Seven reached over to flip on the radio. It was a country song he'd never heard before. He only half-listened to the words. The beat was what interested him the most. It matched the fast, pounding rhythm of his own heartache.

The streets were choked with traffic, turning the twenty-minute drive he'd promised his grandfather into thirty minutes. He didn't mind. It gave him a little extra time to grapple with his melancholy and get it back under control before he had to face another human being again.

Skip Colburn's home had an interesting story behind it. Located on the outskirts of Houston, it was one of those old homesteads that had been passed down for generations. The city had crept closer each year, surrounding the fifty prime acres of real estate with traffic, noise, and high-rise buildings. However, Skip had turned down every offer to buy him out at fair market value. Unless the U.S. Government played the eminent domain card, he was there to stay.

He was stubborn alright, but his stubbornness was one of the things Seven admired most about him. After being wounded in the line of duty and medically retired from the Texas Rangers, he'd continued to scratch out a living on his farm — growing his own crops, raising a few chickens and cattle, drinking fresh well water, and mostly staying off the grid. He didn't own a television or a computer, and he preferred candlelight and open windows over ceiling lights and central air. The only technology he employed on a regular basis was the cell phone he used to call Seven. And Tiff, apparently.

Seven turned down his radio the moment he reached the long gravel driveway leading to Skip Colburn's farm. He had to stop about fifty yards away from the house to wave at a security camera and wait for Skip to open the long metal gate stretched across the lane.

He drove through copses of oaks, cedar elms, and redbuds. In a few places, the fences were in need of repair, and one long elm branch had come down on the edge of the road. From the angle it was sitting at, it looked as if his grandfather had dragged it there to get it off the road. However, he hadn't yet gotten around to sawing it into logs to add to the woodpile by the house.

They were chores he usually saved for Seven on those rare occasions Seven could carve out the time for a little handyman work. He hoped to high heaven his grandfather wasn't expecting him to fire up the chainsaw this evening. He hadn't taken the time to change out of his Texas Rangers uniform yet.

Skip Colburn's farmhouse jutted against the distant sunset. Parts of it were over a hundred years old, and it had been added on to countless times. In places, one could see where the weathered cedar shake siding met the newer cedar shake siding. It was in desperate need of a new coat of stain.

Seven was pretty sure he saw a loose shingle up on the porch roof. He made a mental note to get up there and hammer it down soon. If he didn't, the ceiling below it would leak during the next rainstorm.

He drove around the gravel circle drive and parked. Leaping down from his truck, he whistled for Goliath to hop down behind him. Recognizing the venue, Goliath gave a joyous bark and took off across the side lawn.

"Make yourself at home," Seven called after him, knowing the dog would be safe to roam here. He was too well trained to stray beyond the outer fence row.

As Seven jogged up the porch steps, he discovered a loose board. He mentally added it to his growing to-do list. Hurrying across the wrap-around porch, he followed his nose to the back veranda, where the smoky scent of BBQ filled the air.

His grandfather was lounged in an Adirondack chair that was as weathered looking as the rest of the house. Though he merely nodded at Seven, his expression brightened.

Since he didn't reach for his cane and push to his feet, Seven could only assume his bum leg was giving him a fit this evening. "You doing alright, sir?" He strode across the porch to lift the lid of the grill and turn the steaks. Man, they smelled good! Up to this very moment, he didn't think he was going to be able to work up an appetite this evening. He was wrong.

"I'm not the one you need to worry about." His grandfather's voice was gruff with concern.

"If I don't, then who will?" Seven countered lightly.

"You may have a point," the older man grumbled.

"So, my secret is out." Seven didn't see any point in beating around the bush. "I'm a complete failure as a husband."

"Nobody said that." A scowl wrinkled his grandfather's brow.

"I just did." Seven lowered the lid on the grill and folded his arms. "Go ahead and say what you've gotta say."

"I plan to after you sit." Skip Colburn picked up his cane and used it to point at the chair next to him.

Seven sat. It felt unexpectedly good to take a load off. He rested his Stetson on one knee and tipped his head back against the chair, wishing he could spend the rest of the night there on the porch — just him and the western stars.

"You need to do that more often."

Seven swiveled his head to look at his grandfather. "Do what?"

"Stop. Slow down. Rest."

Just hearing his grandfather's words made Seven yawn. "No argument there."

"And after you get some rest, you need to get back to fighting for your marriage."

Here it comes. Seven's moment of drowsiness disappeared. "I don't know where to even start."

"Do you still love her?"

"Of course I do!" he exploded. "She's my wife, Pops! The only woman in the world for me." It made his heart ache all over to put his feelings into words. Tiff was irreplaceable.

"Then that's where you start. You tell her that. Exactly what you just said to me."

Seven stared in confusion. "She knows I love her."

"You sure about that, son? When was the last time you told her?"

"When she was walking out the door earlier."

"Sounds like you waited too long." Skip Colburn slapped a hand through the air. "Or didn't say it often enough when you had the chance."

You think I don't realize that? "Well, you know what they say about hindsight," Seven growled.

"I don't care what the experts say, and neither does your wife. All she needs to hear right now is that you love her. Say it every chance you get. And don't worry about whether she says it back. She may need time to cool off first."

Seven shook his head, feeling like he was missing something. "I still don't understand why she left. It makes no sense."

"I'm sure she had her reasons, son."

Seven half-rose from his chair as an alarming thought struck him. "Do you think there's someone else in her life?" The very idea made his blood run cold. His job had kept him away so much, he had no idea who she spent her time with these days.

"No." His grandfather looked at him like he was crazy. "No way! How can you say such a thing?"

Finding the man's words oddly comforting, Seven slid back in his seat. "Uh, maybe because she just left me?"

"It's only temporary. You're going to get her back."

"How can you be so sure?" Seven tasted the bitterness of defeat. He hadn't come here looking for false assurances.

"Because I feel it in my gut. You two are right for each other. Don't ever doubt it. That's the main thing I wanted to tell you this evening."

Seven was almost disappointed to hear there'd be no forthcoming ranting and raving, because it's exactly what he deserved. "She's gone, Pops. She doesn't want me to call or anything. Said she needs her space."

"Then give it to her, but don't stop loving her. There's something awfully powerful about a man who keeps loving a woman when he no longer has a reason to."

Seven snorted, unable to follow such garbled logic. "I'll always love her, because she's Tiff. I don't need any other reason."

His grandfather pointed gleefully at him with both hands. "Now, that's what I'm talking about. That's what it's going to take to win her back."

Wishing he shared even half the man's confidence, Seven stood and turned the steaks again. "Dinner's ready."

Like he'd promised, Skip Colburn had diced vegetables and steamed them in a cocoon of foil.

They were resting beside the meat on the grill, camp-fire-style.

Seven loaded up a pair of plates, knowing he would have never been allowed to do such a thing if Tiffany was around. She would have insisted on using glass plates for dinner and arranging each entrée just so on the plate. When she was finished serving a meal, it looked more like artwork than food.

Such were the trials of living with a chef. Seven's heart twisted painfully beneath his ribcage. As much as he'd teased her about her pinkies-up style of food preparation, he missed it already. Greatly. Almost as much as he missed her.

Trying not to think about her fancy dinner plates and the silly green garnish she decorated them with, he handed one of the paper plates to his grandfather. Then he returned to his seat with his plate. As they dug in, he announced his plans to give up his slot at the Texas Hotline Training Center.

"Now why would you go and do a fool thing like that?" His grandfather fiercely shook his fork in the air.

"Because I can't afford the tuition." Seven felt no need to share how Tiff had drained their savings on her way out the door. It was his problem, not his grandfather's. He wasn't looking to beg or borrow money. The only reason he'd mentioned the training center was because his grandfather had a right to know about his change of plans.

"Then apply for a loan or a scholarship. I didn't raise you to roll over and play dead when things got tough."

A scholarship, huh? Now that his grandfather had brought up the topic, Seven did recall reading something about scholarships in his original application. It was probably long past the deadline for applying for such funds, but it might not hurt to look into it. "We'll see." He'd rather not get his hopes up.

"The answer is no if you don't ask," his grandfather pointed out sagely.

"True."

Goliath barked somewhere in the distance. He'd probably found a squirrel or some other small critter to chase. Seven was just glad to hear him again and know he was nearby.

"And after you get that search and rescue certification under your belt, you'll win that wife of yours back and bring her here to the farm." Skip Colburn pounded a fist on the arm of his chair. "Nothing in the world like fresh air, fresh water, and fresh garden vegetables to improve a marriage. Mark my words."

Seven raised his eyebrows. "You want me to bring Tiff here?" *To your rundown farmhouse in the middle of this overgrown wilderness?*

"Why not?" His grandfather shrugged. "It'll all be yours soon, anyway."

Seven was momentarily struck speechless.

When he finally recovered his voice, he muttered, "Wasn't aware you were going anywhere, sir."

His grandfather cackled. "Well, I won't be here forever."

"All the same, I'd appreciate you sticking around a while longer." Seven glanced away, not wanting the older gentleman to witness his pained expression. "You're all I've got left."

"Not true." His grandfather no longer sounded like he was smiling. "You still have Tiff. I know it doesn't feel like it right now, but you do."

CHAPTER 2: COLLISION COURSE

TIFFANY

Tiffany's car coughed and choked like it was on its last leg as she traversed the streets of the gated community where her mother lived. Between the rows of apartments and condominiums, perfectly manicured medians were bursting with flowers. When she finally pulled up to the curb of her mother's brown and red-brick condo, her car motor abruptly died.

That can't be good. Wondering if it would start again when she was ready to leave, she reached for her red leather crossbody purse. It felt way lighter than it had when she'd tossed it on the passenger seat.

Oh, snap! She stared in dismay at the contents of her purse that were scattered all over the seat and floorboard. Also, lying on the floorboard was the all-important white envelope containing her and Seven's life savings. Her hands shook at the realization she must have forgotten to zip her purse shut. It was crazy careless of her, considering how much money she was toting around right now. She must have also been blubbering too loudly while she was driving to hear the noise when her purse tipped over and everything went flying out of it.

Her only comfort was that it was one mess she could easily clean up — unlike the one she'd made of her marriage.

The look on Seven's face when she'd walked out of their apartment an hour ago had almost made her lose her resolve and go flying back into his arms. Almost. Thank God she'd come to her senses before doing anything else stupid. Begging him to forgive her for all the mistakes she'd made during their marriage, most of which he knew nothing about, wouldn't solve anything. The kindest thing she could do for him right now was to get out of Dodge. Hopefully, her troubles would follow her instead of him, and one of them would finally be free of it all.

Seven had seriously looked like he was about to break, though, when she rolled her suitcases past him, which had brought her dangerously close to the breaking point herself.

If there was any other way she could have handled things, she would have. She had wracked her brain for months for a way out of all the money trouble she'd gotten into, but she'd been unable to come up with a better plan than leaving Seven. She was two snaps away from single-handedly wrecking the guy's career as a lawman.

Filing for a legal separation was the only way she could keep Seven safe right now from the trouble skidding in her direction. That was the plan, at any rate. She'd already informed the loan shark who'd been hounding her that she was in the middle of a divorce. Yeah, she'd sort of lied about that detail, but only because she was trying to protect her husband. She'd additionally promised the shark that she had a small settlement coming from the divorce and that she was applying it in a lump sum against the balance she owed the woman.

Yep, the shark was a female. A petite, diminutive woman in a navy blazer and white blouse, she looked more like a librarian than a money lender. It was an image carefully crafted to inspire trust, though she deserved anything but. Tiffany didn't even know her name. All she knew was that she owed her money — lots of it.

Hence, the five thousand dollars she'd removed from her and Seven's joint savings account earlier today. The shark was insisting it be delivered in an unmarked envelope to the usual drop-off point this evening. Tiffany had been making monthly payments on her debt via a set of storage lockers at the airport. She never knew which one until after she arrived. A tiny silver charm in the shape of an infinity symbol was always dangling from the keyring of the one the shark had picked out before her arrival.

But first, Tiffany had a dinner date to keep with her mother. *Lord, give me the strength to get through it without strangling her.* She loved her mother dearly, but the woman had a way of driving her absolute bat cakes with all her silly habits and not so silly superstitions.

Wiping the dampness from her cheeks and taking a deep breath, Tiffany opened the door and stepped out of the car. Moving around to the passenger side, she quickly scooped up the contents of her purse, zipped them back inside, and looped the red leather handle over her head.

The movement caused her to momentarily duck her head and glance down, which served as a guilty reminder of the forty-five dollars she'd spent last week on the pair of black yoga pants she was currently wearing. They boasted a wide support panel in the middle, designed to mask a few extra pounds. As messed up as their marriage was right now, she hoped Seven had liked the way she looked in them.

He'd never been big on handing out compliments. The most words he'd ever spoken all at one time had been on her way out the door earlier — when he'd said he hoped she found what she was looking for, and he hoped it was him.

Replaying his passionate outburst in her mind made her start weeping all over again. "Seven," she whispered brokenly. She wasn't looking for happiness anywhere else, because she'd already found it with him. She could only hope and pray that he would still be waiting for her to come home when she finished resolving her financial troubles once and for all.

Her mother threw open the front door of her condo as Tiffany stumbled her way blindly up the sidewalk. "Baby!" she cried, running down the steps with her arms outstretched. "Oh, my lands! I can't believe what that foolish cop has done to my precious girl."

"Please, Mom," Tiffany mumbled against her plump shoulder, "let's not talk about him." The mess her marriage was currently in wasn't Seven's fault. Not even close. She'd only made it look that way to protect him.

"Well, what else is there to talk about?" Her mother squeezed her tighter. "Did he or did he not just toss you out of your own home?"

"Mom," Tiffany warned, "it's been a long day. Can we please, please, *please* talk about something else?"

"I'll try." Ros Becker dug out a tissue as she stepped back. Stuffing it in her daughter's hand, she muttered, "It won't be easy, but I'll try. Come on inside, baby." Her blue eyes were as puffy and red-rimmed as Tiffany's, and her hair was fast escaping from its bun. It hung in fuzzy ringlets around her temples and cheeks, making her look a decade younger than her forty-eight years. The white apron she had on was spattered with tiny orange spots.

Tiffany was betting it was spaghetti meat sauce from the scent of it as she followed her mother past the fire engine red front door. Her stomach rumbled with hunger as her keen nose picked out the sauce's key ingredients — onion, tomato, garlic, and basil. The last item likely had come from her mother's windowsill herb garden.

Tiffany's fine-tuned chef schnozzle also picked out a different scent, that of freshly baked pasta. Her mother was a baker by trade, so she never, ever served store-bought bakery items. If biscuits, dinner rolls, croissants, wontons or even pasta were on the menu, one could bet their boots they were made from scratch. Her mouth watered just thinking about the imported olive oil, sea salt, and stone-crushed wheat flour her mother preferred to use.

Though her mother's condo was small, she'd spared no expense on furnishings. The overstuffed loveseat was real leather, the globes of her stained glass lamps were custom designs from a local glass-maker, and the mirror over her mantle was edged in roses made of Swarovski crystal. Like her daughter, she had expensive tastes. Unlike her daughter, she could afford to indulge them.

Tiffany had found out the hard way just how dangerous it was to own things she couldn't afford. It was downright scary to think of how sweetly and innocently she'd been lured down the wrong path — in her case, by the desire to be the most beautiful woman in the room on her wedding day.

"Lemonade?" Her mother interrupted her reverie by holding up a frosty crystal pitcher filled to the brim with pink lemonade. Fresh raspberries floated across the top.

"Yes, please." Tiffany gratefully accepted the chilled flute her mother filled. The woman prided herself on treating every meal like it was a five-star dining experience. It was no wonder her only daughter had grown up loving food and food preparation as much as she did.

While her mother returned to the stove to serve up a pair of perfectly arranged plates of pasta, Tiffany sipped on the delicious juice, striving to empty her thoughts of all negativity, if only for a few minutes. After glancing down at the gold-embossed beverage napkin her mother had slid beneath her glass, however, it proved to be an impossible task. Her mind inevitably roved back to the fateful event that served as the catalyst for her current financial troubles.

She'd never forget the gold-embossed message that had sucked her down the tantalizingly dark hole of debt. It had come in the form of a hand-addressed invitation in the mail. She could still see her name scrawled out in flawless calligraphy on the envelope. *Tiffany Rosalea Becker*. Inside was an invitation on ivory linen card-stock. It looked a lot like a wedding invitation, come to think of it. The invitation was for an appointment at a wedding dress shop. At the time, Tiffany had assumed she was meeting with one of the employees who worked there. She couldn't have been more wrong.

It was the shark who'd been waiting for her. It was the shark who'd painstakingly guided her through the process of selecting the perfect (and wildly expensive) wedding dress. It was the shark who'd then offered one hundred percent financing for it on the spot. All Tiffany needed to do was agree to a set of easy monthly payments — discrete cash payments, as it turned out, so her new husband would never have to know just how much she'd splurged on her wedding dress.

The shark had followed through with every one of her promises. The wedding dress was everything she said it would be — real silk and lace edged with real seed pearls. The payment plan was also exactly as the shark had promised. Tiffany's payments had come due every last Monday of the month like clockwork. Tiffany spent the entire month stealthily saving her next payment in cash. She'd stashed it in a shoebox in the back of the closet she'd shared with Seven.

Everything went without a hitch right up until Memorial Day arrived on a Monday like it did every year. Though the airport had remained open and the storage lockers available, no little silver infinity charm had been waiting for her on the locker designated for her payment. Nor had the shark responded to a single one of her frantic messages until the next day, when Tiffany was stiffly informed she was a day late on her payment. That was when she'd discovered that payments which landed on holidays were due the Friday before. Despite her tearful pleading over the misunderstanding, the shark had applied every penalty promised in the fine writing.

The most severe penalty had included the dissolution of their previous zero-interest payment plan. Not only had Tiffany suffered an immediate and exorbitant hike in the interest rate on her loan, she'd also become saddled with the obligation to pay it retroactively to the start date on the note. She wasn't one hundred percent clear on the other penalties that had been applied that day. In the end, all that mattered was that her eleven thousand dollar loan had quickly become a fifteen thousand dollar loan. *Sheer highway robbery!* Following a second late payment, she'd gotten stuck with yet another avalanche of penalty fees. Her monthly payments had increased, too, and were becoming harder and harder for her to scrape up without raising Seven's suspicions.

To make matters worse, the shark was now making noises about some final deadline that Tiffany had no memory of agreeing to. Exactly one month from today, the balance of the note would come due, whether she had the funds available or not. The shark additionally claimed she would be holding both Tiffany and Seven jointly accountable for the final payment now that they were married. Apparently this, too, had been in the fine writing that Tiffany had overlooked, and it was a big problem. Seven could end up in some serious trouble with the Texas Rangers if they ended up defaulting on the loan.

So much for the discrete cash payment plan she and the shark had worked out more than a year ago! Holding Seven jointly liable for anything, just because they were married, was why Tiffany had panicked and filed for a legal separation. That, and because Seven's grandfather had recently confided in her that he was in the process of adding Seven's name to the deed on his farm.

Tiffany shivered at the thought of the shark attempting to file a lien on their farm.

"You're awfully quiet over there," Ros Becker complained, glancing over her shoulder at Tiffany as she put the final touches on their dinner plates.

"Sorry." Tiffany guiltily took another sip of the raspberry lemonade she'd all but forgotten was sitting in front of her. "I'm just...you know..." *Not in the mood*.

"I understand. No need to explain." Her mother's voice was infused with sympathy as she sailed in Tiffany's direction with a plate in each hand. Setting one of them down in front of her daughter with a flourish, she announced grandly, "Dinner is served in the main dining gallery."

Tiffany chuckled despite her misery. "We're sitting on bar stools," she reminded.

"Which is now the main dining gallery at your mama's bee-you-tee-ful hacienda." Her mother broke into a little dance in front of her stove, rocking her ample figure to the beat of the tune inside her head. "I got sick and tired of seeing all that space go to waste, year in and year out. Nobody uses formal dining rooms anymore." Her voice adopted a secretive note. "Not in a million years will you guess what I did to mine."

Tiffany glanced pointedly at the pale gray wall separating the kitchen from the dining room. "It's you we're talking about, so I'm not going to even try to guess." Her mother was too impulsive to predict.

"Truer words were never spoken. How about you save me the trouble of explaining and go see it for yourself?"

Thankful for the momentary diversion from her troubled thoughts, Tiffany slid from her stool and moved across the room. Peeking her head around the corner, she found herself staring at an enormous indoor spa. "Mom!" She stepped into the former dining room in order to get a better look. "You didn't!"

"Oh, but I did, baby girl!" Her mother had always dreamed of owning a spa. However, she'd gone so many years without one that Tiffany had assumed it was only talk.

Wrong. The proof was sitting right smack in front of her. The lid of a brand new spa was pulled back, revealing a pool of water with enticing bubbles rising from a submerged ozonator.

Her mother hadn't stopped there. She'd gone and transformed the entire rest of the room into a tropical paradise. There were faux palm leaves waving against the wall, their bases anchored in brightly painted porcelain urns. Strands of white round patio bulbs had been criss-crossed like Christmas lights across the ceiling. A wicker shelf against one wall boasted a pile of plush white spa towels, tri-folded and stacked at an angle. An unlit sandalwood candle was perched in front of it. On the other end of the table rested a bowl of seashells.

"Wo-o-ow! This is pretty over-the-top." Tiffany's eyes were wide as she returned to the bar.

"It's gorgeous, isn't it?" her mother sighed, pressing a hand to her bosom. "It's like instantly being on vacation every time I step into the room."

Tiffany bit her lower lip. "I don't even want to

know how much all that set you back." The moment the words left her, she wished she could call them back. The last thing she wanted to do was spark a conversation about money, or her own severe lack of it.

Her mother pursed her lips as she carried her plate to the bar and claimed the stool beside Tiffany. "Would you believe me if I said it didn't cost me a penny?"

"No." Tiffany's stomach turned queasy. Everything cost money. "Did you use store credit?"

"Sure did, but only because they offered zero percent financing. The suckers!" Her mother wrinkled her nose in derision.

Tiffany scowled at her. "First of all, going in to debt is never a good thing. Second of all, we both know you can well afford to pay cash for a stinking spa. So, why play Russian roulette with your finances when you don't have to?"

"Russian rou—seriously, Tiffany!" Ros Becker looked aghast. "Because I know your head isn't in a good place tonight, I'm going to ignore your tone of voice along with your assumption that I don't have a clue how to manage my money."

"I'm sorry." Tiffany propped her elbows on the bar and pressed her hands to her face. "You're right. I'm sorry."

"Apology accepted. Sheesh, honey! Zero percent financing really is free money. The longer the store holds the note, the longer I get to collect interest on the funds in my money market account at the bank."

"Until you're late on one measly payment," Tiffany cried bitterly. "Then they stab you right through the heart with a massive interest rate hike and make you pay up big-time." Boy, could she vouch for that!

Her mother sat up straighter on her stool. "Is that why you and Seven are separating? Because of money problems?"

"No!" Tiffany dropped her hands to stare bleakly at her mother, realizing she'd said too much. The concern on her mother's face, however, made her realize that money problems were the perfect explanation for why she was leaving her husband. It was certainly much simpler than explaining the truth. "I mean, yes," she corrected with a humorless laugh. "You know how I like nice things, whereas Seven... oh, my gosh! The man is the world's worst penny pincher." She shook her head. "We fought like cats and dogs every time we balanced the checkbook." It was a lie, of course. Seven had been nothing but generous the entire time they'd been married. He'd faithfully brought every paycheck home and deposited it in their joint account. They'd been living on a shoestring, all so she could finish college while secretly juggling a pile of debt he didn't know about.

Without warning, Tiffany burst into tears. "I've made such a horrible mess of my life," she quavered.

"Oh, baby!" Her mother hastily set down her fork and leaned over to gather her daughter in her arms. "I wish I'd known things were so tight for you guys. If you would have told me sooner, I'd have been glad to slip you some money." Her expression grew hard. "That hard-nosed cop you married wouldn't have needed to know."

Though her mother meant well, her words only made Tiffany cry harder. *I'm such a horrible person!* Throwing Seven under the bus in a conversation with her mother was so unfair to him. He was a good man, one who was foolish enough to keep loving her despite the fact that he deserved a better woman in his life. That dismal thought brought on yet another round of tears.

Her mother gave up trying to get her to eat. "I have an idea," she suggested brightly. "How about we go sit in the spa for a few minutes?"

"Thanks, b-but I can't." Tiffany's lips were trembling, making it hard for her to speak. "I'm not good company right now. I, ah..." She sniffled loudly. "I should probably just shower and go to bed, since I need to hit the road early."

She'd lied to Seven about her job interview in Dallas. It wasn't coming up like she claimed. It had already happened, and she'd completely nailed it — partly out of desperation and partly out of merit.

And now she was about to become a chef at the renowned Texas Hotline Training Center. She'd even managed to secure one of their staff cabins on campus, which meant her neighbors on both sides of the street would be tough law enforcement officials like Seven.

The loan shark would continue to follow her and keep tabs on her wherever she went, but the woman wouldn't be able to do much to her within such a secure setting. *I hope.*

"I understand, baby," her mother sighed. "If you change your mind, I'll be in the spa."

SEVEN STARED at the screen of the laptop he had balanced on his knees. He was back at the apartment, sitting on his and Tiff's threadbare sofa, trying not to think about the number of times they'd necked there. Since she wasn't there to scold him about his lack of manners, his feet were propped on the coffee table in front of him. He hadn't bothered to remove his boots.

Goliath was sprawled on the cushion beside him with his head resting on his front paws. At one point, he made a whining sound in the back of his throat that told him the dog was missing Tiff.

But not as much as Seven was. With the way he was feeling right now, he might just spend the night right where he was, boots and all. He was exhausted, body and soul. But first, he was going to look up that information about the scholarship he'd talked to his grandfather about.

Before he could open his electronic student application, however, an incoming email pinged its arrival.

The name of the sender caught his attention.

It was from his closest friend in the world, Detective Noah Zeller, a guy he'd spent some time in foster care with back in junior high. It was before Skip Colburn had retired from the Texas Rangers and rescued Seven from the foster system. Well, technically, Noah was no longer a detective. After he'd graduated from the Texas Hotline Training Center a few months ago, they'd offered him a position as an instructor. His fiancée had been offered a job there, too, following the completion of her internship. Seven didn't know much about Farrah Carmichael, other than the fact she was an expert dog handler. Oh, and she made Noah happy. For that reason alone, he couldn't wait to meet her.

The subject line of Noah's email made him smile. It read, *You must be living right!*

Though nothing could be further from the truth, Seven clicked open the email to see what his friend had to say. Scanning the first few lines of the message, his jaw dropped.

Just saw your name on the list of scholarship

recipients and wanted to be the first to congratulate you. Lucky dog! Hope things are better between you and Tiff since the last time we spoke. Really looking forward to seeing you at the training center next month!

Seven swung his boots to the floor and sat up so quickly that he nearly dropped his laptop. *What list? What scholarship?*

As if sensing his excitement, Goliath raised his head and gave two sharp barks.

It took Seven a few more minutes of scrambling to find the notification email from the Texas Hotline Training Center. It had arrived two days ago. *Unbelievable!* As it turned out, Noah wasn't kidding. Seven had been awarded a full-ride scholarship to the training center. The email included a list of sponsors for the various scholarships they awarded, along with a notation as to which one had sponsored Seven's. It was a company by the name of Infinity. He'd never heard of them, but he didn't care. He would look them up after he graduated and kiss the ground their employees walked on.

Accompanying the scholarship were a few forms he had to sign electronically in order to accept the offer.

Yeah, baby! Seven was excited enough to howl at the moon while he affixed his initials to the bottom of each form. There were three full pages of writing he probably should have read first, but he was in no mood to wade through a bunch of complicated legalese.

Scholarships were free money, baby! Everyone knew that. As he signed the last page with a gleeful flourish, he reached over to scratch Goliath's ears. "This is good news for both of us." He would be required to train with a search and rescue dog, so Goliath would get to attend the training with him.

We're going to the Texas Hotline Training Center! There was no need now to call the Admissions Department in the morning to cancel his slot. Nor was there any need to cancel his leave paperwork with the Texas Rangers. He hadn't taken any time off since he'd gotten married, so he had plenty of paid vacation days saved up.

I'm actually going to the training center!

CHAPTER 3: MOTHER-IN-LAW FACTOR

SEVEN

One month later

By the time Seven's report date to the Texas Hotline Training Center rolled around, he was like a horse champing at the bit to get started. The past month had been the most excruciating one in his adult life. After a single text from Tiff telling him that she'd accepted some chef position in Dallas, there'd been no other communication between them. She was pretty skimpy on details about the job and didn't respond to his text back, where he'd asked for the name of the company she was working for.

Come on, Tiff! Talk to me! Though he'd agreed to give her space, her radio silence was killing him. He remained in a constant state of worry about her safety. His only comfort was that his month of training at the Texas Hotline Training Center would place him in the same vicinity as her. He'd visit every blasted restaurant in Dallas if he had to. One thing was for sure, he wasn't returning to Houston until he laid eyes on her again and saw for himself that she was alright.

The evening before his drive to Dallas, Seven picked up his mail one last time, locked up his apartment, and drove with Goliath to his grandfather's place. They would spend the night at the farm and take off in the morning. Though he'd packed light for himself, the rear cab of his truck was loaded down with an impressive amount of dog supplies — a cage, two enormous bags of dog food, and an assortment of training gear. Goliath wasn't inside his cage, of course. He much preferred to ride shotgun, ogling every car and passenger they passed.

Despite Skip Colburn's blustering to the contrary, Seven changed into his work boots shortly after his arrival and knocked out some much needed yard work. As usual, Goliath took off to roam the distant fields while Seven worked. He mowed about an acre in the front yard and another acre in the back. Then he pulled out his grandfather's chainsaw and trimmed a few trees. The guy had done a little fiddling with the fallen limb on the side of his driveway, but most of it was still there, and Seven was tired of looking at it. He finished cutting it into logs. It took three trips with the wheelbarrow to cart all of them to the woodpile next to the house. Afterward, he buckled on a tool belt and dragged out an exten-sion ladder to have a closer look at the loose shingle he'd noticed a while back.

His grandfather thumped down the porch steps with his cane and craned up at him from the base of the ladder. "Whatcha doing up there, son?"

"Thought I saw a loose shingle. Did you see any leaks during the last rainstorm?"

"Nope."

"Ah. Here it is." Seven located the shingle in question and was able to slide three gloved fingers beneath it. It had probably come loose during the 30 mph winds and golf ball-sized hail that the area was notorious for during the spring season. He quickly tacked it back into place with a few roofing nails.

"Glad you noticed it." Skip Colburn treated Seven to one of his rare grins that was mostly hidden by his shaggy gray beard. "Your eyes are much younger than mine." His favorite pair of red suspenders was holding his jeans over his gaunt hips.

Seven had never been good at accepting compli-ments. "What else do you need done tonight, Pops?" Knowing he was going to be absent for an entire month made him anxious to knock as many items off the to-do list as possible.

"Nothing I can't handle on my own. You already took care of the big stuff."

Seven scowled in concern at him as he climbed

down from the ladder. "What about that creaky porch step?"

"Already fixed it." His grandfather gave him a matter-of-fact nod. "I'm not entirely useless, you know."

"I'm going to be out of town for an entire month," Seven reminded. "If you need something done, now's the time to say something."

At his grandfather's stubborn silence, Seven added gruffly, "Don't want to spend my whole time there worrying about you, too."

"There's no need for that, son." His grandfather reached over to clap a hand on his shoulder. "I'm going to be just fine. What I need is for you to wash up and meet me out on the back porch. I've got the grill going and company on the way. And before you pitch a fit about the company, may I point out that you already would've known about it if you hadn't spent the past two hours drowning out my every attempt at conversation with all your lawn mowing and hammering."

"Can't say that I'm in the mood for company." Seven's scowl deepened. "I was hoping it was just going to be the two of us this evening."

"Well, too bad, because she's already on her way."

"She?" Seven's interest was piqued. "Who are we talking about?" His heart pounded at the possibility that Tiff had come to pay his grandfather a visit.

"It's not someone you're going to be all that happy to see, so how about we just leave it at that?" Without giving Seven a chance to respond, the elderly man ambled in the direction of the grill, leaving his grandson staring curiously after him.

Roger that. We have an unwanted guest on the way. Seven didn't have any enemies that he was aware of, so he had no idea who his grandfather was referring to. Shaking his head, he put away the ladder and headed inside to shower and change. If he was going to be forced to socialize with someone he wouldn't be thrilled to see, he certainly wasn't going to dress up for the occasion. He'd be wearing sneakers and basketball shorts, thank you very much!

A wave of nostalgia hit him as he threw his suitcase atop the queen-sized bed in his old bedroom. He was glad he was spending the night here before departing. Though he'd moved out a few years ago, it still felt like home.

Shrugging on a navy t-shirt, he strode to the window overlooking the side yard. Beyond the area he'd mowed was a fenced in pasture. His grandfather no longer tended a full herd, but he kept a pair of dairy cows for the milk and a half dozen beef cattle for the steaks, tenderloin, and jerky. To the east of the pasture was a modest-sized garden where his grandfather grew just enough to stock his pantry and cellar. He no longer produced large crops to harvest and sell. Once upon a time, he'd employed a staff to help him out with tasks like that, but no longer. He considered himself to be retired from all that.

Seven gazed out the window, arms crossed, longing to return the property to its glory days. He'd never gotten to see them, and Pops didn't talk much about them. Seven could only assume it was too painful a topic. After losing his daughter and son-in-law in a helicopter crash and his wife to cancer shortly afterward, Pops had all but shut down the farm. He'd buried himself in his work as a Texas Ranger for the next twelve years, right up to the point when he'd taken a few live rounds on the job and been forced to retire. At that point, he'd hunted down his only living relative, a scrawny grandson who'd been traded from one foster home to the next, and finished raising him on his own.

Though Skip Colburn had never been very warm and fuzzy, Seven thought the world of him and had followed in his footsteps after high school to become a Texas Ranger. It was an honorable job, chasing down heinous criminals to help make Texas a safer place to live. However, being a lawman wasn't a cakewalk. The toughest thing about it wasn't the dangers he faced nearly every day. The toughest thing was what little time his choice of careers had left him to be a husband to Tiff.

He'd meant what he said to her about doing

whatever it took to get her back, even if it amounted to a job change. She'd never made a secret of the fact that she wanted to start a family.

So do I, Tiff. He stared into the distance. "Please, God," he muttered, "give us one more chance." Whatever had gone wrong between him and his wife, he knew it was going to take a miracle to fix it. But Pops was right about one thing. Tiff would love it here on the farm. If — no, *when* — he won her back, he was going to run the idea past her.

The sound of tires against gravel alerted him to the fact that his grandfather's mysterious guest had arrived for dinner. A few seconds later, a knock sounded on the front door. Jogging down the hallway and through the living room, he reached the foyer and opened the door.

To his amazement, Ros Becker was standing on the other side. She had on one of her favorite floral tunics, and her dyed blonde hair was twisted atop her head in a complicated knot. Though her gaze was spitting anger, her blue eyes reminded him of Tiff's — so much so that for a moment he could hardly breathe.

"Ms. Becker," he said stiffly, wondering why she, of all people, was standing there. Then it hit him. She was the dinner guest his grandfather had promised he wouldn't be too happy to see.

She rolled her eyes at his greeting. "Oh, for crying out loud, Seven! You're married to my daughter. Or were. Don't you think it's time to lay aside formalities and be frank with each other?"

He stared at her, unable to remember a time when she'd been anything but brutally frank with him. "Tiff and I are still married, ma'am."

Though her nose seemed to be permanently wrinkled in his direction, something akin to relief sparked in her gaze. "That'll certainly make what I came to say a little easier." Without waiting for an invitation, she swung her apple-shaped figure through the doorway with a nimbleness that belied her size. He stared after her as she made a beeline for the exit at the end of the hallway that ran the length of the house.

What you came to say, eh? He followed after her, shaking his head and wondering why she hadn't just circled the wrap-around porch instead of cutting through the living room.

The back door was open, and only a screen door separated them from the porch. Ros Becker peeked both ways through the screen, then turned around to face him. She slapped her hands on her hips, making her cluster of silver bracelets jangle. "Your grandfather is busy at the grill. That should give us a few minutes to talk."

He paused and eyed her warily. "About?"

She drew a sharp breath. "So, you're going to make me spell it out, are you? I'm talking about all the debt you and my daughter have gotten yourselves into, that's what! I know the first year of marriage is hard for every married couple, but I honestly expected more financial discipline out of a son-in-law with a law enforcement degree. Including one who was foolish enough to taunt the Fates by marrying my sweet baby girl on Friday the thirteenth."

What debt? All Seven could do was stare at her, utterly dumbfounded. Since she seemed to be expecting a response, he finally muttered, "Honestly, ma'am, I have no idea what you're talking about." He and Tiff weren't in any debt that he was aware of.

"This isn't the time to play dumb, Seven. I'm really worried about her."

"That makes two of us, ma'am." He still had no idea what she was talking about.

"Call me Ros, for crying out loud!" she snapped. "I meant it when I said it's time to drop the formalities between us." She jammed the sleeves of her tunic higher up her arms before slapping her hands back on her curvy hips. The gesture made her look ready for battle.

"Fine, Ros, but I still have no idea what you're talking about."

Her forehead furrowed into deeper rows of indignation. "I'm talking about whatever zero-interest loan you defaulted on that has my daughter worked into such a lather."

He shook his head, feeling a headache begin to

gnaw at the back of his skull. "I think there's been a misunderstanding. Tiff and I aren't in any debt." It had been a tough first year of marriage, full of financial sacrifices on both their parts, but staying out of debt was their reward for keeping their bootstraps so tight.

"She says you are." Ros continued to glare at him. "I know you and I haven't always seen eye to eye when it comes to making my daughter happy, but if I had any idea you were having money problems, I surely would have done something about it. I still will, if it'll bring my baby back into town where she belongs."

"We're not in debt," he repeated flatly. "We share a credit card for gasoline and groceries, but we pay it off every month. That's it." He glanced away as he continued, "She deserved better than that hole-in-the-wall apartment we've been living in, but it was only supposed to be temporary. We were going to buy a house as soon as we could afford it." After she finished college. After they had a chance to save a small nest egg. After they had the opportunity to get more established in their careers. Unfortunately, Tiff had left him before they'd gotten through even half of that checklist.

Ros slowly lowered her arms to her sides, looking perplexed. "But she was so specific about the details." She waved a hand uncertainly. "About when you missed a payment, how the interest rate hiked to some astronomical level and how it feels like one big horrible trap that you're never going to get out of and..." Her voice dwindled on a helpless note.

As Seven listened to her, it slowly dawned on him that Ros was repeating an actual conversation that had taken place between her and her daughter, a conversation that might finally shed some light on why his wife had subsequently filed for a legal separation.

"Ros." He surprised them both by stepping forward and reaching for her shoulders to gaze intently down into her worried features. "I need you to repeat everything you can remember about what Tiff said." He paused a moment before adding, "Please."

She wilted beneath the seriousness of his tone. "You truly don't know anything about the loan she was so upset about?"

"Nope." He shook his head, his gut tightening with apprehension. "This is the first I'm hearing about it."

"Oh, dear heavens!" Ros murmured. "What has my precious baby gotten herself into? No wonder there was such a dark aura hanging over her head the last time we were together!"

Seven didn't believe in omens and auras, but he figured that was Ros's way of saying Tiff had been upset. "What exactly did she tell you about the loan?" His mind raced over the possibilities, but he couldn't come up with any answers on his own. There'd been no trail of clues. No indicators. Whatever was going on with Tiff, she'd done a blasted good job of hiding it from him. But why?

"Did she happen to tell you when she took out the loan, how much it was for, or why she needed it?" He hated the fact that his voice had slipped into what Tiff called interrogation mode, but he couldn't help it. In times of crisis, this was how he operated — peeling back the details of a case and painstakingly examining each one.

"No, no, and no!" Ros moaned. "All I can tell you is that it sounded like a lot of money." She squeezed her eyelids shut. "Oh, my lands, Seven! How could I have been so blind?" She swayed on her feet. "I knew there was something terribly wrong the last night she was in town. She came to my house, you know, after leaving you."

He nodded grimly. "I am aware."

Anxious tears shimmered in his mother-in-law's eyes. "I figured she'd come home to vent about the horrible man she'd married, so I made a few scathing remarks about you to get the conversation started." She sniffled damply. "Lord, have mercy! She about bit my head off for it. Call me crazy, Seven, but I'm beginning to think that whatever made my daughter decide to leave town wasn't about you, after all."

Despite the fear choking him on Tiff's behalf,

Seven experienced a curious burst of hope at his mother-in-law's words.

A shadow crossed the screen behind her head. "What's going on in there?" Skip Colburn barked.

"I-I..." Ros's voice shook, and she was unable to finish her thought.

"You might as well bring the conversation outside," Seven's grandfather growled. "I agreed to let you talk to the lad, but not to browbeat him to death inside my own home." He yanked open the screen door and ushered them toward the porch.

Keeping his hands on his mother-in-law's shoulders, Seven gently led her outside. Passing up the Adirondack chairs, he deposited her on the porch swing instead.

He shot his grandfather a warning look on their way to the swing. "Easy," he instructed beneath his breath. "I've got this."

His grandfather's silvery eyebrows shot toward the ceiling, but Seven didn't stop to explain. Whatever Ros had to say next was too important to risk sidetracking her.

He took a knee in front of her. "Ros, if Tiff is in some sort of trouble, I need to know." His mind continued to race over the possibilities. It was only a three-and-a-half hour drive to Dallas. By all that was holy, he'd be making that drive tonight, just as soon as his mother-in-law finished spilling her guts.

She spread her hands, looking scared. "I already told you everything I know, Seven."

"Tell me again," he instructed crisply.

She shrugged. "It was a zero percent financing deal. She was either late for a payment or missed a payment, and the interest rate went up. Way up. Oh, and she said it was retroactive to the beginning date of the note." She frowned. "Was it a student loan, do you think?"

"No way." He shook his head. "We made those payments together. I can personally vouch for the fact that she graduated without any student debt." *That I am aware of.* A sick feeling settled in the pit of his stomach at the thought that she could've taken out a loan without telling him. Tiff wouldn't have been foolish enough to do something like that, though, would she? She was too smart and too level-headed. However, it had been a tough year finan-cially for them. They'd squeezed every dollar to make it go as far as they could.

Though the two of them were far from wealthy, he unfortunately made just enough with the Texas Rangers to keep her from qualifying for any federal grant money. Due to losing her father during high school, her grades had suffered to the point of not qualifying for many scholarships, either. In hind-sight, Seven had been so fixated on staying out of debt that he might have inadvertently pushed his wife into doing something stupid during a weak moment.

What have you done, Tiff? Seven wished like crazy that he'd just supported his wife's original request to apply for a student loan. Sure, they would have had a loan to pay off after she graduated, but they would've been able to eat something other than PB&J sandwiches and chicken noodle soup throughout the past year.

Another thought struck him, making him whip out his cell phone for a quick internet search of credit score companies. Finding a reputable company, he tapped his way through their application screen and ordered a free credit report for himself. Then, because he happened to have all of Tiff's personal information memorized, he did the same for her. To his disappointment, a message popped up on the screen that the reports would be sent to him within fifteen days. That wasn't going to help him answer any questions this evening.

"What are you doing?" Ros asked nervously.

He lifted his phone and turned it around so she could see the screen. "I just ordered credit reports on both Tiff and me. It could take a couple of weeks to receive them, but it'll tell me if there any outstanding loans under either of our names." If there was, it would give him a starting point for digging further into the matter.

"That's pretty clever of you." Cautious hope

warred with the apprehension in his mother-in-law's waxy features.

He grinned without humor. Clever was far from the way he felt at the moment, more like a complete failure as a husband. "That's the nicest thing you've ever said to me," he noted dryly. "Any chance you'll say it again, so I can record it?"

To his dismay, tears started to roll down her cheeks. She nodded fiercely. "I'll do that and a lot more if you help me get my daughter back."

Another thought gripped him. "Do you know where she is?" he asked quickly.

"You don't?" Ros sounded incredulous.

He hated to admit it, but no. He didn't. "All I know is she took some job in Dallas. She was a little light on the details." Seven ran a hand over the lower half of his face as he pocketed his phone again. "Said she needed her space, so I've been trying to give it to her."

"It's near Dallas, I suppose." She pursed her lips. "Somewhere on the outskirts."

"Ros, where is my wife?" It sickened him to realize he might've visited every restaurant in Dallas in the coming days and never located her.

She studied him in troubled silence for a moment. "Some place safe." She sounded a little less certain as she added, "For now."

His grandfather chose that moment to thump his way loudly in their direction with his cane. "We had an agreement, Ros. My grandson has answered all of your questions. Only seems fair that you answer a few of his."

She threw up her hands. "In case you can't tell, I'm caught between a rock and a hard place here. My daughter specifically instructed me not to tell anyone where she was going."

"I'm still her husband," Seven reminded.

"And a police officer, to boot," his grandfather snarled. "Seems to me if your daughter is in the trouble you seem to think she's in, you might want a guy like Seven on your side."

"You're right." Ros Becker sniffed again. "I can only hope my baby girl will forgive me for breaking my word to her, since I promised..." Her voice dwindled away on a gusty sigh.

Seven leaned closer, willing her to hurry up and spill whatever she knew about her daughter's whereabouts.

"She's working as a chef at some police academy." Ros cocked her head at him. "You probably know more about it than I do. According to her, they teach search and rescue stuff."

Seven's jaw dropped. "Are you, by any chance, referring to the Texas Hotline Training Center?"

"Yes." Her nod was vehement. "That's the place. I take it you've heard of it?"

"Yeah. You could say that." Feeling dizzy with

relief, Seven glanced over his shoulder to get a reading on his grandfather's expression.

Skip Colburn looked ready to break into a jig.

"Listen, ah..." Seven turned back to face his mother-in-law. Reaching for her hand, he informed her, "It just so happens I'm reporting there in the morning for a month of training." And by tomorrow morning, he meant tonight, but she didn't need to know that.

"Oh, no!" she cried, looking horrified. "You can't, Seven. She was adamant about you not finding out where she was. She made me promise." Tears gathered in her eyes again. "I honestly don't know what she'll do if she finds out I broke my word to her. She wasn't in a very good place the last time we spoke. What if..." Her lips trembled. "What if she takes off running again? Then none of us will know where she's at."

"You're right." He hated to admit his mother-in-law was right about anything, but she might have a point. The last thing Seven wanted to do was crowd Tiff so much that she took off again.

"Okay." He clenched his jaw. "I won't tell her I'm coming, and I won't contact her after I get there." Not right away, at any rate. "I'll continue to give her the space she asked for." He would keep an eye on her from a distance, though, while continuing to dig into the loan situation. She'd eventually figure out he was at the training center. By then, he'd hopefully have more information about what trouble she was in. Lord willing, he'd have a solution to offer by then as well.

"Promise me, Seven." Ros Becker gripped his hand like a lifeline.

"I promise." He squeezed back.

"And don't step on any sidewalk cracks while you're there," she added quickly, "or look into any broken mirrors, or—"

"Got it!" he interrupted, hoping to distract her from her laundry list of superstitions. "I'll make you one more promise while I'm at it. I'm going to fix this, and I'm going to get my wife back." His gaze narrowed in warning. "And when I do, you're going to bake me the pie of my choice and endure my presence for an entire meal without tossing a single insult my way."

Ros made a face at him through her tears and pretended to consider his request. "Not a single one?"

He shook his head at her, giving no ground. "Green zone status for one full hour. Those are my terms."

Ros gave his grandfather a scathing look. "Are all son-in-laws this difficult, or just mine?"

"Going once, going twice." Skip Colburn's eyes twinkled. He was enjoying taunting her.

"Oh, all right!" Ros rolled her eyes and gave a

long, drawn-out sigh as she gave Seven a thumbs up. "Deal."

―――――

WITHIN THE HOUR, Seven was rolling down the interstate toward Dallas. Goliath, who'd been a bit of a job to round up from his run through the fields, was back in the passenger seat. He smelled like dirt and grass, which meant he'd been digging and rolling in it.

"You're making a mess over there," Seven grumbled, eyeing the dusty paw prints the dog was leaving on the seat.

Goliath gave a happy bark in response, tongue lolling as he took in the lights and sounds of the traffic surrounding them. As usual, he was wiggling with excitement about being in the truck as opposed to being left behind.

Seven snorted. "That didn't sound like much of an apology."

His phone buzzed with an incoming call. The caller ID was listed as *Unknown*. He considered ignoring it, since it was likely spam. However, he had a long drive ahead of him. On the outside chance it was a legitimate call, he decided to take it. His phone hooked to a holder mounted to his dashboard, so it was easy to reach up and connect the call on speaker phone.

"Who's this?" he asked without preamble.

"Well, hello to you, too!"

He instantly recognized the booming voice on the other end of the line. "The answer is still no." It was a buddy of his from high school, Easton Whitlock, though most of their friends simply referred to him as East. He'd left the Texas Rangers a few years back to start his own security firm. Though Seven had always suspected it was because he was too much of a hothead to spend the rest of his life taking orders from others, there were days he honestly envied the guy.

"Down, boy!" East teased. "I wasn't calling to recruit you tonight, though the offer remains open. Wide open, in case you had any doubt."

"Then what do you want?"

"Right to the point." East chuckled. "You never were one for small talk, were you?"

"Aw! Would you rather chat about the weather first?" Seven mocked, ducking his head to glance up at the sky. "Let's see. It's partly cloudy with no chance of me ever trading in my current dreamy hours and pay to report to a joker like you."

"Shoot, Seven!" A note of exultation rang in his friend's voice. "Sounds to me like you've actually given it some thought."

"Very little, so don't get your hopes up. You won't be bossing me around anytime soon."

"Who said anything about bossing you around?"

East exploded. "I was thinking more along the lines of a partnership."

Seven, who'd been half-listening up to this point to the country song playing on the radio, did a mental double take. "Wait. What?"

"Partner, as in partner. You heard me, bro. I've got more contracts rolling in than I can handle. Sorry if I sound like I'm bragging, but I'm bragging. Business is good, but I'm going to have to start turning away customers soon if I don't get some help."

Seven was impressed and a bit envious. "That's great for you, East. Really."

"Uh, no. It's not." East sobered. "I just finished admitting that I'm about to start turning business away."

"Sounds like a nice problem to have." Seven's voice came out drier than he intended, but he couldn't help it. Unlike his friend, he had real problems to worry about.

East blew out a breath. "Speaking of problems, I was really sorry to hear about Tiffany leaving. That's the real reason I'm calling. I just found out, and man! Made my stomach hurt."

Seven scowled at the phone. "So, now you're keeping tabs on my personal life, too?"

"Eh, get over yourself." East sounded disgusted. "This isn't about work, and you know it. We were friends long before we decided to pin on our badges."

"I don't need your pity."

"Oh, for crying out loud, Seven! All I wanted to say was, I'm here if you need anything."

"I don't, but thanks." The pain of Tiff's leaving was too fresh to talk about it. Seven was still too raw.

"I mean it. You give me the green light, and I'll help you dig up any dirt you need on anyone."

Seven snickered despite the scummy element to the offer. "I really don't think she's cheating."

"You don't sound one hundred percent sure, either."

"Let it go, East. I'm heading to Dallas for a month of training at the Texas Hotline Training Center. I wouldn't have time to spy on my wife, even if I wanted to." Which he did. Badly. But he didn't want to risk losing her forever by doing something so stupid.

"Fine. This is me, letting it go, but I stand prepared to pick up this conversation again if—"

"It won't be necessary," Seven interrupted firmly.

"If you say so." East didn't sound all that convinced. "Well, good luck at the training center. Gotta run. I'm getting another call." He clicked over to it before Seven had a chance to respond.

Seven disconnected the line, shaking his head at his friend's unexpected mention of a partnership. It wasn't the worst idea he'd ever entertained. The guy operated on a short fuse sometimes, but he was a real go-getter. And if the mansion he lived in and the flashy sports car he drove were any indication, his new business venture was a profitable one.

Maybe following his training at the training center, he would give Easton Whitlock a call back to see how serious he was about that partnership gig.

CHAPTER 4: RED LETTER DAY

TIFFANY

Tiffany rolled out of bed before daybreak on the last Monday in July. A mixture of dread and excitement churned in her belly. Today was a double whammy. The next batch of hungry students would arrive at the Texas Hotline Training Center, expecting three square meals per day from the cafeteria she ran. But that wasn't all. Today was also the day her final loan payment was due, which meant it was going to be a very long day, indeed. At the end of her work shift, she would be renting a car and making the three-and-a-half-hour drive back to Houston.

She padded barefoot to the bathroom in the private cabin she'd been living in on campus, grateful that the powers-that-be had approved her request to live on the street the staff fondly referred to as Instructor's Row. Though she lived alone, she felt safe, surrounded by neighbors who were former soldiers, police officers, and other first responders.

Staring at her reflection in the mirror over the vanity, she grimaced at how gaunt her face looked. For the first time in her adult life, she was dropping weight without even trying. Her pants were loose, and her shirts were downright baggy. A woman who loved to cook and eat, she was forever fighting an extra ten to twenty pounds, but not any longer.

A few months ago, she would have been over-joyed to achieve her current size. Instead, she found it to be depressing. The woman staring back at her in the mirror was too pale, too unhappy, and too lonely. This wasn't how she'd ever wanted to lose weight. She hardly recognized herself.

She brushed her teeth and applied a minimal amount of makeup, rushing through the tasks to avoid looking at the stranger in the mirror any longer than she had to. After dressing in the center's stan-dard black cargo pants and combat boots, she left her white chef's jacket off a little longer. She did her final preparations for the workday in a simple white tank top.

Since there was no one around to care what kind of housekeeper she was, she didn't bother making her bed all the way. All she did was yank the quilt over her pillows before leaving the room. Sliding a card-board cup under the coffee dispenser, she brewed a single cup, wishing she had a reason to brew a second one. However, Seven wasn't here to share it with.

She missed him like crazy. After a month away from him, her anger and frustration over all the late nights he worked was growing fainter and fainter. Her strongest memories were the good ones. She missed how he looked when he returned home after his shift — the way he always untucked his shirt before he finished walking through the door, the way his evening shadow scraped her chin when he gave her his honey-I'm-home kiss, and the hungry look he got the moment he smelled whatever she'd prepared for dinner. Gosh! She even missed tripping over the boots he kicked off in the middle of the living room.

Maybe someday soon they would get to bicker over stuff like that again, but she needed to get through today first. Snapping a plastic lid over her cup of coffee, she took a few bracing sips before tackling the last item on her before-work to-do list — double checking the amount of cash she'd prepared for her final loan payment.

She hadn't slept worth a hoot last night. The one time she'd managed to doze off, she'd dreamed she was late on her final loan payment. As a result, the loan shark had sprouted a few extra rows of teeth and literally devoured her. Tiffany had awakened on a yelp of horror, sat up in bed, and been unable to go back to sleep.

She nervously withdrew the precious white

envelope from her purse on the kitchen table. Opening its flap, she carefully counted out the dollar bills one last time to make sure she'd enclosed the correct amount. In addition to the five thousand dollars she'd withdrawn from her joint account with Seven, she'd included her entire first paycheck, the money she'd cleared from selling her car, and — *God, forgive me!* — the funds the pawn shop had given her for her wedding ring.

Seven might never forgive her when he found out she'd hocked her own wedding ring, but she had no choice. It was the only other asset she'd had left to squeeze money out of.

Because of the exorbitant interest rate on her loan, the interest due was nearly as high as the principal amount. Once she made her final payment, her wedding dress would be paid for nearly two times over. *Worse investment of my life.* The experience had all but ruined her memories of her wedding. She was more than ready to put the entire sordid ordeal behind her and get on with the rest of her life. More importantly, she was anxious to begin the painstaking process of fixing her marriage — assuming that Seven would be willing to take her back at this point.

In the meantime, she had over a hundred students and staff to feed while keeping a smile pasted on her face and pretending that everything was alright.

Even though it wasn't.

I can do this. I have to do this. She carefully tucked the flap of the envelope shut and placed it back inside her purse. It was time to put on her game face. Unlike the rest of the staff, who wore solid black uniforms, she and her associates in the cafeteria got to wear pristine white jackets over their cargo pants. Though her uniform pants and combat boots were a far cry from what chefs typically wore at other dining establishments, Tiffany loved her uniform. She was crazy proud of the fact that she'd climbed this far up the ladder in the restaurant industry at such a young age. Yeah, it was a cafeteria job, not a high-end restaurant position. However, to be serving as the head chef of any place at the age of twenty-five was a major accomplishment. No doubt her brand spanking new culinary arts degree had helped pave the way, along with the glowing recommendation she'd received from the world-renowned chef she'd interned with in Houston.

As she buttoned her white jacket over her white tank top, she silently vowed that she would break her silence with Seven and give him a long-overdue call later this evening — but only after her loan was paid in full. Even if he wasn't ready to forgive her and jump straight into reconciliation, she knew she owed him an explanation for the events leading up to their separation.

She was, quite frankly, surprised that he'd taken

her request for space to such lengths. Yeah, she'd asked him for space, but she hadn't expected his silence to be so, well, deafening. Normally, he texted her a half dozen times throughout the day and called her as soon as he hopped in his truck to head home. All too often, though, his texts and calls were merely to inform her that he was running late. Or that he wouldn't be making it home, after all, due to some last minute crisis at work. She'd lost count of the number of all-nighters he'd pulled during their first year of marriage.

As hard as those nights had been, though, nothing had been harder than Seven's complete radio silence this past month. She missed him so much that it hurt. She seriously couldn't remember the last time she'd looked forward to anything as much as she was looking forward to calling him this evening.

Hugging that thought to her chest, she stepped outside her cabin at the crack of four. Though the skies were still dark, moonlight poured whitely over her tiny porch and front yard. She locked the front door, shoved her hands in the pockets of her jacket, and hurried down the porch steps. Ducking her head against the wind, she trudged the mile or so to the kitchen that adjoined the cafeteria.

She could tell by the balmy breeze that it was going to be another warm day. As she sauntered past the dog kennel, she could have sworn she heard

Goliath barking on the other side of the wall. How she missed Seven's search and rescue dog! He'd warned her not to get too attached to the Doberman — that Goliath was a work dog, not a house pet — but that had proven to be an impossible task. It was love at first sight between her and Goliath. His soulful brown eyes had captured her heart, along with his playful attitude and boundless energy. In some ways, the dog was like the child she and Seven had not gotten around to having yet.

Wincing at the memory of how close they'd come, she pressed a hand to her flat belly. For the hundredth time, she wondered if it was normal to miss a human being she'd only carried inside her body for a few weeks. She'd lost the pregnancy during one of Seven's extended work shifts. For reasons she still didn't understand, she'd been unable to tell him about it upon his return home. He'd been so tired and drained. So had she. Instead, she'd waited until he'd gone to sleep and silently wept the rest of the night on her side of the bed.

Three months later, however, it wasn't any easier to think about it. She was still grieving the loss of their baby like it was yesterday. That was something else she needed to tell Seven about. Maybe not tonight, but soon.

With a sigh, she pushed open the back door to the kitchen and let herself inside.

Her sous chef glanced up from the chrome

preparation counter in the middle of the room. "Whoa! What's up?" He was busy rolling out biscuits, his dark fingers dusted with flour.

She scowled at her tall Black partner in crime. "Good morning to you, too, Marcel. It's way too early for guessing games, so if you've got something to say to me..."

He shook his shaved head at her. "Just meant you're rocking the death-warmed-over look this morning." He had the build of a linebacker, which made him look like he meant business, even with something as innocuous as a rolling pin in hand.

"Gee, thanks," she muttered, too tired for verbal sparring. "When I come up with an appropriately insulting comeback, you'll be the first to hear it."

"I mean it, Tiffany. I'm worried about you." Marcel paused with the rolling pin suspended over the dough in front of him. "By worried, I mean my boss at my last job was a complete rear end, and I'm not anxious to lose you to whatever has you so..." He shrugged. "Well, like this."

As she passed by him on her way to her office, she leaned closer. "Keep rolling. In case you haven't seen the memo, the commander has decided he wants fresh biscuits and all the trimmings in the foyer outside the main auditorium this morning."

By trimmings, she meant butter, jam, gravy, scrambled eggs, bacon, and ham. Essentially, the commander had ordered a last-minute continental breakfast for his latest batch of incoming students.

"I got the memo, boss lady." Marcel went back to rolling dough. "The ham is in the oven, and the eggs are cracked and stirred, ready to be thrown on the stove the moment Jamal arrives."

Jamal was their most junior chef on staff, a wiry Hispanic fellow with a ready smile whom they could always count on to pick up the slack. To her knowledge, he'd never been late, not once called in sick, and always got his work done. They had a few other employees who helped out at the serving line. They were a small crew but a mighty one, which she in no way took for granted.

"How could I ever live without you guys?" Though she kept her voice light, she meant every word.

"Clearly, you can't." There was a long-suffering note to Marcel's voice. "Which brings me back to my original concern."

"No, it doesn't," she said firmly. "My personal life has nothing whatsoever to do with the topic of food preparation."

"Okay, fine. I'll go for the less subtle approach." He grimaced at her. "You were wearing a wedding ring the day you showed up here, and now you're not. Does that mean you're free to attend the staff appreciation dinner with me this evening?"

"I'm still married." She gave him a warning look.

"I'm also still your boss." Not that she was planning on attending the dinner, anyway. Her plans in Houston weren't the kind she could easily get out of.

He looked pointedly at her bare left hand. "So the ring—"

"Is in the shop," she cut in hastily, not bothering to specify that she was referring to a pawn shop instead of a repair shop. She'd begged the owner to hold on to it for a few weeks to give her a chance to buy it back. He'd refused to make her any promises.

"In that case, I'll stop by the cabin of my bossy friend around seven o'clock to drive you there, seeing as you're also no longer in possession of the car you arrived at the training center with."

"Omigosh, Marcel!" She spun around to stare at him in irritation. "You sounded so much like my husband just now." She stopped and bit her lip, having said more than she intended.

"Because he's tall, dark, and handsome like me?" he prodded.

"Actually, I was referring to the not-so-subtle interrogation thing you have going on." She rolled her eyes at him.

Marcel's expression sharpened with interest. "So, he's in law enforcement?"

"He's a Texas Ranger, Mr. Nosy Pants," she snapped.

"Bummer!" He went back to rolling out biscuits more vigorously than before.

"How is that a bad thing?" she demanded, not sure what had gotten into her sous chef this morning.

"Because you said it like he's a real person, not just some cover story."

"He is real." For some reason, the confession made her burst into tears.

"Whoa!" Marcel cried again, tossing aside his rolling pin and striding in her direction. "I didn't mean to make you cry. I was just testing the waters before I said or did something stupid. You know, like asking you out." He reached her and enclosed her in a bear hug. "You give off such confusing vibes sometimes."

"It's complicated," she sobbed, clinging to him. She knew it wasn't very professional of her, but he was the closest thing she had to a friend at the training center.

"You can say that again." The coldly familiar baritone carried across the kitchen, making Tiffany stiffen in alarm.

"Seven?" she gasped. Wrenching herself free from Marcel's embrace, she turned to face her husband. "What are you doing here?"

Good gracious, but he looked amazing in his hard Texas Ranger sort of way! She drank in his blue eyed glower beneath the brim of his favorite black Stetson, supremely uncomfortable at being the brunt of such an accusing look.

This wasn't even close to how she'd imagined

their next meeting going. She had on almost no makeup and was as skinny as a scarecrow. Plus, she could only imagine how many ways her weeping fest in Marcel's arms might be misinterpreted.

"Interrupting something, apparently." The hardness of his voice didn't come close to masking the pain in his expression.

She hated knowing she was the cause of it. She also hated how thin he looked beneath his faded plaid shirt and stone-washed jeans. Like her, he'd lost some weight, something she could probably take credit for.

"You're not interrupting anything," she stated flatly. "I'm just having an extremely bad day." She smoothed her hands nervously down her white jacket, struggling to staunch the rivulet of tears dampening her cheeks. "Seven, this is my sous chef and right-hand man, Marcel Craft. Marcel, this is the Texas Ranger I was telling you about a few minutes ago — my husband, Seven Colburn."

Her reference to him as her husband made some of the tension leave Seven's shoulders. He ignored Marcel's outstretched hand. "Can we talk?" he inquired of her. Anger flared in his gaze as it flickered briefly back to her sous chef. "Alone?"

"Of course. My office is this way." She glanced over her shoulder at Marcel as she marched doggedly toward it. "Keep the biscuits coming, please. And when Jamal arrives, have him man the stove."

"Aye, aye, captain." Marcel gave her a floury salute and went back to work.

She could feel his dark, curious gaze burning a hole between her shoulder blades as she opened the door to her office. Stepping inside, she flipped on the light and waited for Seven to join her.

He stalked into the small room behind her. "So help me, Tiff, if you don't tell me what's going on—"

She hastily shut the door behind them. "Marcel asked me out on a date," she confided in a shaky voice as she moved to her desk and tossed her purse on top of it. She bent forward to turn on her computer. "I told him I'm married. End of story."

"There seemed to be a little more to it than that, but I'm not talking about your sous chef." Seven stalked across the room after her. "Yet."

"Oh." She stared at him blankly for a moment, still processing the fact that he was at the training center — standing right in front of her in her office. "Why are you even here, Seven? I thought we agreed to give each other some space."

"Two reasons. The first one is because I was accepted into the training center's Urban Rescue Program. I'll be starting this morning."

"Holy golf balls!" She pressed a hand to her racing heart, completely broadsided by his revelation. "When did this happen?" Sadly, it underscored just how little they'd been communicating with each other lately.

His jaw tightened. "I applied months ago and was accepted, but I asked them if they would postpone my attendance and give me a later slot. Didn't think it was the best time to leave you for a month. Didn't think it was appropriate to even mention to you that I was thinking of leaving you for a month, everything considered." His voice turned bitter. "Of course, that was before I knew you were toying with the idea of leaving me for good."

Every word he spoke felt like a slap. "Seven, I haven't left you for good," she cried.

"Really? Because that's the way it feels," he growled. "You don't text. You don't call. For the past month, I had no idea where you were living or if you were even alive. But far be it from me to ask, because I'm sick and tired of being accused of invading your precious space."

"I…" She didn't know what to say in her defense. Until she paid off that blasted loan, she wouldn't be in the position to tell him the truth, not without dragging him into the mess right along with her. A sudden thought struck her, making her shiver. "How did you know I was here?" She wrapped her arms around her middle, feeling miserably exposed. If Seven could find her this easily, then others could, too, like the loan shark.

He spread his hands. "Look, I ran into your mom last night. When she found out where I was headed today, she let it slip that you were in the area." He grimaced. "I don't think she meant to tell me. She was mostly busy informing me how bad of a son-in-law I've turned out to be."

"That's not true," Tiffany said quickly. As irritated as she was at her mother for sharing her whereabouts, she was glad it was Seven who found her and not someone else.

Seven scowled at her. "What did you say?"

"You're no worse of a son-in-law than I am a wife." She bit her lower lip. "Mom will never admit it, because she has a big blind spot where I'm concerned, but I think you and I both know it takes two to fight."

"I didn't come here to fight," he assured her in such a clipped tone that her heart sank. He certainly didn't sound like he'd come to reconcile, either. He dug in his pocket and produced a much wrinkled red envelope, which he slapped down on the desk in front of her. "This is the only reason I'm standing in your office right now. Right up until I read this note, I had fully planned to keep my head down the entire month and leave without you ever knowing I was here."

"What's this?" She stared at the red envelope in puzzlement. Though it was addressed to her, he'd already torn it open and presumably read it.

"It came in the mail yesterday, but I didn't get around to opening it until this morning."

"You opened my mail?" She was taken aback.

Even while they were living together as a married couple, he'd never been one to nose through her things.

"Honestly? I didn't pay any attention to who it was addressed to. I was just drinking coffee and opening mail to make sure I didn't forget to pay any bills before my training starts." His mouth twisted. "After reading it, though, it didn't sound like something I should ignore. So, at the risk of making you mad all over again, here I am."

"I'm not mad at you. I just...need my space," she mumbled absently as she withdrew a note on white card stock.

"So you keep saying."

Her eyes rounded on the note's gold embossed lettering. "Oh, no!" Her hands started to shake as she sank into her swivel chair. "Not again." It was another invitation. For tonight. Apparently, she wouldn't be dropping off her final payment in an airport storage locker like she'd done every month before now. Instead, her presence was expected at the same bridal shop where it had all began — after hours. From what she could glean, she was expected to come alone.

"Tiff?" Pressing both palms flat on her desk, Seven leaned forward to reclaim her attention. "Talk to me."

"I can't." She dragged in a sobbing breath as she

stared at the horrid piece of paper. "This is some-thing I have to take care of myself."

He drew a deep breath and glanced away from her, jaw working. "Is there somebody else in your life, Tiff?"

Yes! But... "It's not what you're thinking." Her voice shook.

"You have no idea what I'm thinking right now," he growled.

"I want to." Her voice trembled. "But not today. Please."

"Fine." He pushed away from her desk. "Just do what you have to do, and get it over with. I'm tired of not knowing when I'll see you next or where we stand with each other." He gestured angrily between them. "I won't do this forever."

CHAPTER 5: DOG CUSTODY

SEVEN

Tiffany flinched as if he'd slapped her. Shoving the invitation back in its envelope, she tossed it on her desk and stood.

His gaze latched on to her left hand, noting that she was no longer wearing her wedding ring. He glanced away, unable to bear the sight of the empty spot where the white gold ring had once rested. It looked wrong and felt wrong.

When he glanced back at his wife, she was holding her hand behind her back. She'd noticed that he'd noticed her missing ring. "I only need a few more days," she informed him quietly. "Then we'll talk. I promise." Her expression was pale but resolute, indicating that her usual brand of stubbornness was very much back in place.

He ignored the sudden stab of longing to march around her desk and take her in his arms. Call him crazy, but he adored her stubbornness and grit, the way she'd always given her college classes and intern work one hundred percent of her finest efforts. It was how she'd landed the position she was currently filling. He was insanely proud of her and wanted nothing more than to tell her that. There was another part of him, though, that wished she'd apply more of her stubbornness to making their marriage work. Instead, here they were, walking on eggshells around each other, hardly knowing what was safe to say next and what wasn't.

"In case you've forgotten, I'm going to be busy for the next few days," he reminded her coolly. *Make that the next few weeks.* There were no guarantees they'd find a better opportunity than now to chat prior to his graduation.

"Very busy, from what I understand." She gave him a faint smile as she smoothed a hand over her hair. She had her blonde tresses pulled back in a French twist at her nape. "It's a tough school, but it's nothing you can't handle."

"Uh, thanks." Her fervent vote of confidence caught him off guard. "I wasn't expecting a pep talk."

"It's not a pep talk." She slowly walked around her desk. "So, ah...is there any chance you brought Goliath along with you?" The wistfulness in her voice made him scan her features in speculation.

"Of course I did." Goliath would be his canine

partner for the duration of the search and rescue training program. "Why?"

Her wistfulness faded to an expression of indignation. "Because he's like the child we never had."

His eyebrows shot upward. "You mean the one you walked out on a month ago?"

"Don't be cruel, Seven." She glared at him. "You know I've always adored Goliath to pieces. Shoot!" She sniffed. "If I'd filed for a divorce from you instead of a separation, we'd be embroiled in a custody battle over him right this second." Her chin lifted in defiance.

He stared at her in disbelief. "The money you took wasn't enough, huh? You'd fight me for my dog, too?"

"That's not fair," she snapped. "I said I'd pay the money back. And, yes. I would fight you tooth and nail for joint custody of our precious baby."

Baby? His eyebrows stretched higher. "He's a dog," he reminded flatly. "I'm not sure there's any such thing as sharing joint custody of a dog." He found the notion oddly amusing, however, and downright welcome. He was probably a fool for getting his hopes up, but he liked the idea of maintaining some sort of ties with Tiff, even if it was only through a stinking dog. He glanced at his watch, knowing he had to go. His orientation ceremony in the DCSRA Auditorium was beginning in less than fifteen minutes.

"Well, it should be," Tiffany muttered in a dark voice, watching his movements. "Guess we're out of time to argue the matter."

At that moment, his stomach let out an obnoxiously loud growl of hunger. He met her gaze, feeling sheepish.

She broke into a laugh. "Some things never change."

He searched her expression, liking the sound of her laugh. "Some things don't need to change." He wasn't one of those people who was allergic to change, but he wasn't the least bit happy with the way things stood between him and his wife at the moment.

"On that, we agree." She sauntered toward her office door and opened it. "Quick. There's something I want to show you."

He followed her from her office, shooting a quick glance around the stark office they were leaving behind. She hadn't hung anything on the walls or put out a single picture frame. It was hard to tell if it was the office of someone who'd just arrived or someone who didn't plan to stay long. Either way, the bare look of it was troubling. Tiff had always been an exuberant decorator. This wasn't like her.

She led him back to the kitchen where Marcel was still working. He was finished rolling out dough and was busy taking large pans of biscuits out of the oven as the timers beeped. He nodded at Seven as he filled two enormous bread baskets full of the fresh-baked bread.

Seven nodded back, though he accompanied the nod with a warning look. He wasn't quite ready to forgive the guy for finding his wife in his arms a few minutes ago.

"Here." Tiffany reached around Marcel to pluck one of the biscuits from the basket. She tossed it in Seven's direction.

He caught it in mid-air, delighted to find it was still warm.

"There will be plenty more of these in the lobby after your orientation ceremony. My team and I will be setting up a continental breakfast there while you're inside the auditorium receiving your first set of marching orders." She stepped closer to him and dropped her voice so that he alone would hear what she said next. "I hope one is enough to tide you over."

"For now it is." Despite his undeniable hunger, eating breakfast was the least of his concerns. "Last question before I go." He kept his voice low like hers. "Are you heading back to Houston this evening for that shindig at the bridal store?"

Her face paled. "I'm thinking about it."

The way her eyes dilated and her breathing became uneven, he was taking it as a yes. It was equally obvious that she was afraid — so afraid that he could almost taste her fear while standing this close.

As angry as he was about the state of their marriage, his concern for her was stronger. "Alright, then. Drive safe."

She blinked at his words. "Um, about that." She stepped closer to him and hissed, "Is there any chance I can borrow your truck this evening?"

He snorted in disbelief. "Really, Tiff?"

She bit her lower lip. "Well, I figured you won't be needing it for a few days, and—"

"Where's your car?" he interrupted.

"Never mind." Her face reddened. "It was a stupid question that I had no right to ask. I don't know what I was thinking."

"Maybe you were thinking we're still married." He withdrew his keys from his pocket and held them out to her. "And on some level, you realize there's nothing I wouldn't do for you. Even now."

Her lips parted, and an agonized sound escaped her. "Thanks," she whispered. Their fingers brushed as she took the keys from him.

"Listen," he reluctantly backed away from her, "if there's any time at all in the next few days, I'll take a look at that ignition on your car."

She shook her head at him, blinking rapidly. "That won't be necessary."

Oh, but it is, darling. She'd let him get closer than he anticipated this morning, close enough to feel her fears and uncertainties. His policeman instincts were reading them like a cry for help. He was going to do everything in his power to answer that cry, even if it meant giving up a whole blasted night of sleep to fix her blasted car.

Whatever it takes, Tiff. I'm going to fix us. Another glance at his watch told him he had a mere five minutes left before his report time in the auditorium. Letting himself out the side exit, he quickly scarfed down the biscuit Tiffany had given him. Then he whipped out his phone and dialed East Whitlock, not really expecting him to pick up.

"Yo!"

Seven gave a silent chuckle of gratitude. "I need a very big favor."

"Huh. Guess that makes two of us."

"I'm serious, East."

"Me, too."

"I think my wife is in trouble."

"Listening." East's voice grew coldly serious.

"I have to be somewhere in three-and-a-half minutes, so I'll make this quick." As he jogged in the direction of the auditorium, he rattled off the address of the wedding shop Tiff had been invited to. "For reasons I do not understand, my wife has been invited to meet with someone there after regular store hours this evening." He stated the exact time.

"I'll be there early and stay late," East assured quickly.

"She can't know you're there."

"Figured that. Anything else?"

"Yeah. Whatever's about to go down has her all hot, bothered, and cagey. My gut says it has something to do with why she left me."

East groaned, "I hate to point out the obvious, bro, but it's a wedding shop and the two of you are separated. Maybe there's another guy in the picture."

"Then you'll be digging through dirt, something you once claimed you were really skilled at."

"Yep. I'm the best."

"Add it to my tab."

"Or," East countered, "you can come work with me. Having each other's backs will be one of the perks."

"I don't have time to get into that right now."

"Then I'll take an IOU for a future sit-down."

"Okay. You win." Seven was too desperate for East's help to continue haggling. Not to mention, he was out of time. "Gotta go."

"Don't worry about Tiff. I'll have eyes and ears on her the entire time."

"Thanks." Relief shot through Seven, taking the edge off both his worry and exhaustion.

"You're welcome, partner."

Seven disconnected the line, grinning like a moron as he reached for the door of the auditorium and stepped inside.

TIFFANY HAD a hard time meeting Marcel's gaze as she washed her hands and joined him at the preparation counter. They worked in silence for a while, filling baskets, gathering paper products and plastic ware, and setting out an array of silver buffet servers.

"I'll have the eggs, ham, and bacon ready in a jiffy!" Jamal sang out from his station at the stovetop.

"You're the best!" Tiffany forced a cheerful note into her voice.

"Oh, are we speaking again?" Marcel teased.

"If you insist." She rolled her eyes at him. "I was actually enjoying your silence for once."

"Oo, burn!"

"Sometimes the truth hurts." It felt good to take a bite out of someone. She'd been on edge all morning.

"Yeah, I was thinking the same thing." He shot a sideways glance at her.

She held up a hand. "Don't start in on me. I'm not in the mood to joke, gossip, or beef about my husband."

"So I gathered." He waggled his thick, dark eyebrows suggestively at her. "For a woman I didn't know was married until a few minutes ago, those were some awfully strong emotions zinging back and forth between you and your husband. You gotta admit my confusion is understandable, considering the missing wedding ring and all."

She squeezed her eyes shut against the pain his

words caused. "May we please talk about something else?"

"Sure. What's up with the keys he handed you?"

"Marcel!" she gasped, opening her eyelids.

"Oh, come on, Tiffany!" he exploded. "I made a fool of myself by asking you out only seconds before the husband I didn't know you had walked through the door. I wouldn't mind an explanation."

"It's complicated." There was no way in a million years she could make him understand.

"You didn't look like you were in the middle of a divorce," he prodded.

Right. Knowing she was supposed to be acting more like a divorcee, she pressed a hand to her rapidly beating chest. "Like I said, it's complicated."

"I'll say! He was kissing you with his eyes when he walked out of here. Not exactly the look of a guy wanting the big D." He pulled the lid off the first silver pan as Jamal arrived with the first skillet brimming with scrambled eggs. They jointly scraped their spatulas against the skillet until the fluffy yellow eggs had been transferred to the serving dish.

Jamal's coppery skin and dark curly hair were proof of his Hispanic heritage, while the permanent half-grin quirking his wide mouth was proof of his endless fountain of good humor. "What are you two whispering about over here? Whatever it is, I want in on it."

"Nothing," Tiffany said hastily, shooting a warning look at Marcel.

"Yep, nothing." Marcel shrugged. "You just missed meeting her husband, by the way."

"You're married?" Jamal's grin slipped. "How did I not know this?"

"Oh, where do I begin?" Marcel sang out.

Tiffany shot him a pleading look. "It's complicated." *Pardon me, but I really just wanted a little privacy.* She hadn't counted on being asked out on a date during her first month of work.

"Big D in the works," Marcel explained in a stage whisper.

"Oh, I see what's going on here." Jamal swiveled his head between them with a knowing look.

"There's nothing going on here," Tiffany said firmly. "Other than the fact we have a continental breakfast to cater in the next building over right about now."

The raucous sound of barking outside made their heads swivel toward the door.

"Goliath?" Tiffany would have recognized those barks anywhere. It was a relief to know she hadn't been losing her mind earlier when she thought she heard him inside the dog kennel. Hurrying to throw open the door, she was caught off guard when the Doberman Pinscher came sailing through the opening.

His front paws landed on her shoulders.

"Watch out!" Marcel yelled, sprinting in her direction with the empty skillet in his hand.

"It's alright," she assured, throwing her arms around the dog's middle and hugging him joyfully. "I know him."

Marcel stood there, staring at her in confusion. He kept the skillet suspended in mid swing. "He looks dangerous, Tiffany."

Goliath glanced over at him, baring his teeth to growl a warning.

"He can be, if properly provoked." She shot him an exasperated look. "Put that pan down. It's upsetting him."

"The feeling is mutual." He slowly lowered the pan. "Having a two-ton Doberman in my kitchen isn't exactly the highlight of my week."

Tiffany felt a stab of guilt over the way he'd called it *his* kitchen. They'd been hired at roughly the same time, and she had reason to believe he'd applied for her job in addition to his own. As nice as he'd been to her, she had to assume she was the reason he hadn't gotten his first-choice of positions.

"It was a bit of a surprise to me, too." Inwardly, she was overjoyed at seeing Goliath again. "I'm not sure how he got out of the kennel, but I'm going to lead him back over there. How about you two get started transporting the food? I'll join you in a few minutes."

Marcel and Jamal locked glances.

"Did you hear that?" Marcel demanded dryly.

"Sure did." Jamal cocked his head, pretending to listen. "It's the sound of the buck being passed, brother."

Tiffany gave Goliath another squeeze hug as she lowered his paws to the ground and shooed him toward the door. "Speaking of delegating, I may get a late start in the morning. I have to make a quick run out of town this evening, and I'm not sure when I'll be back."

"Does this mean you're skipping the staff appreciation dinner?" Marcel looked so offended that Tiffany wanted to kick herself. She'd forgotten all about it.

"I'm sorry, but there's a semi-urgent family matter I have to handle," she lied.

"I take it this has something to do with your husband's visit this morning, eh?" Marcel's upper lip curled at her.

"Marcel!" She couldn't believe he was being so nosy. It was like he was trying to trick her into saying more.

"Okay, okay!" He handed the skillet back to Jamal, raising his hands in surrender. "We'll get the food transported while you transport," he paused to grimace at Goliath, "this massive pile of dog fur back to the kennel."

Tiffany didn't have to go far. The moment she

stepped outside, one of the interns from the kennel came jogging in her direction.

It was a dark-haired teen in jeans and braids who looked barely out of high school. "I'm so sorry, ma'am," she gasped, reaching for Goliath's collar. "I don't know what got into him."

"It's alright." Tiffany knew exactly what had gotten into him. He was a smart dog. Somehow he'd figured out that his mama was at the training center, and he'd come looking for her. "He and I are friends."

"Oh, really?" The young woman looked fascinated. "I'm India, by the way." She held out a hand the shade of a chocolate caramel bar.

"I'm Tiffany, the head chef." Careful to avoid stating her last name, she squeezed the intern's fingers.

"Oh, wow! A chef. Again, I'm really sorry that Goliath got away from me."

"It's alright. I think he was just looking for a little attention." Tiffany reached over to scratch him behind his ears.

"Oh, wow!" India said again, her eyes widening. "He's so affectionate for a search and rescue dog, don't you think?"

"It's because he was trained by a volunteer crew," Tiffany explained. "They were more lax with him than the police force would've been."

"I'll say." India watched in amazement as Tiffany bent to kiss Goliath on the head.

"Bye, baby," she murmured. "I'll come pay you a visit soon."

He gave a woof of happiness, as if understanding every word she said.

"Unbelievable," India murmured as she led him away.

CHAPTER 6: THE WEDDING SHOP

TIFFANY

Tiffany returned to her office in the kitchen to run a lint roller down the front of her outfit. She wished she had the time to run back to her cabin and change, but she didn't want to dump the continental breakfast solely on Marcel and Jamal. She had to settle for scrubbing her hands in the bathroom attached to her office and rejoining them in the kitchen.

"That was quick." Marcel eyed her white jacket, as if searching it for dog hair.

"What? Are you allergic to dogs or something?" She hoped like crazy that he wasn't. Otherwise, she might need to head back to her cabin and change after all.

"Nope. Just allergic to any form of contaminants in the kitchen."

She pretended to be offended. "I've been called a lot of things in my day, but—"

"I was *not* referring to you!" He shook his dark head at her, grinning.

"Oh, good," she sighed, pressing a hand over her heart. "For a minute there, I was afraid I'd ruined things between us forever."

"Not true." He lowered his voice as he glanced over his shoulder at Jamal, who'd gone to fetch a tray of ham from the oven. When he turned back to her, his smile was gone. "Listen, ah, I wouldn't mind hitting the reset button on the entire morning. I never meant for things to get this awkward between us."

"It's more my fault than yours." She smiled sadly at him, wishing she'd previously given him some hint about her married status. "But, yes. Let's hit the reset button, please."

"I guess the cat's out of the bag about how I feel about you, though. I'll turn in my resignation if you want." He looked so sick at heart that she reached for his hand.

"No way!" She gave his fingers a quick squeeze. "Resignation denied." The very thought made her shudder.

"That makes me feel a little better. Still feel like an idiot for misreading the situation, but..." He shook his head. "Would it be too bold to ask you to put me on your wait list?"

"My what?" She wrinkled her forehead.

"I'm offering to get in line for when you become single again."

Her mouth fell open. "No way! There's no wait list. You deserve far better than me, anyway. Trust me."

His expression was unreadable as he shrugged. "Not sure I agree with your assessment, but we can circle back to it some other time."

As he bent to place one of the covered server trays on the rolling cart, she caught a glimpse of something gold in his pocket — something that very much resembled a badge. Because she was the wife of a Texas Ranger, she was familiar with a great number of law enforcement badges. Unless it was a trick of the light, the one Marcel was carrying around possessed the eagle topper of an FBI shield.

Which was just plain crazy. *I'm imagining things.* Unless he was into cosplay or something, there was no way her sous chef was carrying a real FBI badge in his pocket. There just wasn't. His chef credentials had to be legitimate for two reasons. Every person the training center hired went through an exhaustive level of screening, and he was an incredible cook in his own right.

He straightened and caught her staring. "Now what? Do I have as much dog hair on me as you do?"

With a squeal of alarm, she glanced down at her clothing, anxiously searching for any dog hair she'd missed. She couldn't find any.

"Made you look," he teased on their way out the door with their trio of food carts.

"You're a truly awful human being," she muttered. "But that's okay, because I always get even."

"Bring it on!" he taunted with a wink.

She chuckled at his antics, dismissing her earlier suspicions about him. He was way too nice and way too flirtatious to be a federal agent.

To her intense relief and equally intense disappointment, Seven kept his distance from her after the orientation ceremony. He and his classmates dove with gusto into the continental breakfast she and her staff had laid out, laughing and chatting amongst themselves.

She, Marcel, and Jamal presided behind the serving table, refilling trays as they were depleted and keeping the area tidy. From her vantage point, she couldn't help noticing the redheaded classmate who was sticking to Seven's side like a cocklebur.

Tiffany watched the woman from beneath her lashes. *A lot of policemen don't wear their wedding rings, you little twit! If you had a clue about how law enforcement officers live their lives, you wouldn't jump to conclusions.*

"They've been separated out into their squads already," Jamal announced in a low voice, interrupting her disgruntled thoughts. "It may look like they're simply getting acquainted with each other, but nothing could be farther from the truth. They know the training center will soon weed out the ones who don't have what it takes to graduate. Which means what we're really watching are secret alliances being made. Unspoken agreements between two-sies and three-sies to stick together and help each other graduate."

"You watch too much TV," Marcel scoffed, wrinkling his nose at their junior chef.

"Am I?" Jamal asked lightly, not looking the least bit offended. He'd been at the training center longer than both Marcel and Tiffany, so she had no reason to doubt what he was saying about how things worked around here.

As far as alliances were concerned, though, she wasn't entirely convinced that graduating was the only thing the students in front of them had in mind. It seemed to her that the redhead in Seven's squad was going out of her way to monopolize his attention for more personal reasons.

Marcel bent his tall frame over Tiffany's to speak against her ear. "I've never met a woman who wears jealousy very well. In case you're wondering, you're no exception."

She made a face at him. "I'm not jealous. I'm just..." There was no word for a woman in her shoes, someone who'd made such a big mess out of a perfectly good marriage.

"Right. You're only imagining every way you can poison the woman without leaving a trace." Marcel nodded in grave understanding.

A chuckle escaped her. "Like I said earlier, you're an awful human being."

"But not wrong." He gave her a knowing nod.

Her lips quirked. "Since you're in charge of our inventories, I'm assuming we don't have any ricin on hand?"

"Not a single grain. Or cyanide or rat poison," he affirmed with a grin. "You'll just have to settle for killing her slowly and painfully inside your head."

Chuckling, Tiffany spared another glance in Seven's direction and found him glowering at her and Marcel. "Now look what you've done," she murmured beneath her breath.

Marcel waited until Jamal was occupied with refilling a serving tray on the other end of the table before spreading his large hands. "He deserves everything he has coming. Any man who's dumb enough to let a woman like you go..."

Remorse zinged through her. "I'm the one who walked away from him," she confessed.

Marcel's upraised eyebrows told her that she'd let him provoke her into revealing yet more information about her shuffling marriage. "Well, he allowed it to happen."

You have no idea what you're talking about.

Knowing he wouldn't understand even if she tried to explain, she sighed and turned her back on him. The weight of Seven's truck keys in her pocket made her white jacket hang a little lower on one side. When she used her spatula to push the remaining scrambled eggs forward in the tray, they gave a muted metallic thud against the plastic table in front of her.

"Want me to skip out on the staff dinner and go with you?" Marcel inquired softly.

She paused her stirring for a second. "You don't even know where I'm going."

"Bet I could figure it out if you let me ride shotgun."

Instead of smiling at his joke, she let out a huff of resignation. "I appreciate the offer, but I need you here. You'll be in charge of the kitchen while I'm gone." She added beneath her breath, "And if I don't make it back."

Marcel was no longer smiling, either. "If you change your mind between now and then, my offer still stands. Just for the record, I'd trust Jamal to cover down in the kitchen for a few hours."

She gave a jerky nod, but she knew she had no intention of employing his suggestion.

MAN, but the past month living apart from Tiff had been tough! However, it was nothing compared to how Seven felt while being forced to stand by and do nothing while she flirted with her sous chef. He clenched and unclenched his fists at his sides while he endured the endless chatter of his only female squad mate. It was hard to pay attention to anything the woman was saying, since he was preoccupied with wanting to swing a fist into the guy's smug choppers.

It didn't help that he was taller, darker, and more handsome than Seven's average height and looks. Seven didn't consider himself to be butt ugly, but he knew he wasn't God's gift to women, either. Only in Tiff's arms had he ever felt like more than average. And now a guy other than him was making her laugh and smile. He wanted to drop to his knees and howl his misery at the ceiling.

His only comfort was that at least she'd be driving his truck later this evening — a seven hour round-trip in a vehicle where her photograph was tucked against the visor and their wedding photo was swinging on a pendant from his rearview mirror. He hoped it made her realize just how much of his head space she still took up.

"So, which city do you hail from?" his redheaded squad mate asked cheerfully. She'd introduced herself as Cecilia. He couldn't remember her last name, but he was very much aware of her fingers brushing his shoulder as she spun around to survey the room full of fellow trainees.

"My wife and I live in Houston," he informed her blandly. "Where are you from?" He couldn't have cared less, but it only seemed polite to return the question.

Her curious green gaze dropped to his left hand. "Oh! You're married?"

"Yep. Still a newlywed. And you?"

She shook her head, her smile fading. "Guess I haven't met Mr. Right yet. You know how it is," she sighed. "Careers like ours don't leave a lot of time for romance."

He didn't say anything, since he had no interest in keeping the conversation going, but he nodded. Unfortunately, he very much understood what she was talking about.

"Sorry." She shook her shoulder-length hair back. "I'm usually a better conversationalist than this."

He arched an eyebrow at her. "I'm still waiting to hear the city you're from."

"Oh, gosh!" she moaned. "I'm boring you to death. Next thing you know, we'll be talking about the weather."

He pursed his lips, noting that she'd never answered his question. "I'd say it's overcast with a chance of dog bites and sleepless nights ahead."

"Right." She let out a peal of laughter as her earlier sunshine returned. "Do I look as nervous as I feel?"

Seven was only half-listening. The other half of him was enjoying the fact that Cecilia's laugh had made Tiff glance his way again. This time, there was no mistaking the sour look she gave the woman at his side.

Moments later, their instructor appeared. He led them outside and placed their squad of eight into a small formation.

"I'm Officer Terrance Belmont," he barked. Like the sous chef who worked with Tiffany, the instructor was dark-skinned and at least six-feet tall. "Take a good look at my mug, trainees. This is the face that'll occupy your nightmares for the next few weeks."

Though several of Seven's classmates chuckled, there was no answering smile from Instructor Belmont. Their humor quickly fizzled.

"You'll run to the kennel in formation to collect your dogs. Then you'll run with your dogs to the urban simulation rubble, where you will await my next instructions. I expect you to be standing in formation when I get there."

Seven felt like he was in his first year at the police academy again. He could handle a bit of hazing, but he hoped their instructor wasn't one of those guys who enjoyed being in charge more than he enjoyed doing his job. It was vitally important to Seven that he leave the training center knowing a thing or two about search and rescue operations.

He soon discovered just how little he had to worry about. Terrance Belmont turned out to be a wealth of information when it came to dealing with any number of emergencies — from terrorist attacks to hostage situations to natural disasters. Not only did he possess the textbook learning, he had firsthand experience as one of the first responders at the Twin Towers on 9/11.

Cecilia's green gaze had gone from interested to downright worshipful after finding out Instructor Belmont had been on the scene during the 9/11 terrorist attacks.

Good luck, Instructor Belmont. Seven silently wished the fellow his best during the onslaught of hero worship he undoubtedly had coming.

Instructor Belmont trained them as rigorously as if the next 9/11 would happen before nightfall. He first put them through three straight hours of scenting and tracking training with their dogs. It started off with standard stuff that both the dogs and their handlers found easy. The training quickly progressed to climbing up the debris and picking their way across the rubble.

One of their classmates sprained an ankle, earning him a trip to the clinic. Seven felt sorry for the guy, knowing it would be exponentially more difficult for him to graduate with an injury. He was going to have a tough decision to make in the next few hours — whether to try and muddle through the remainder of the month in a splint or boot with the aid of crutches, or opt to recycle himself to a later class.

And so their group of eight students became seven like his namesake. They were tired and dirty by the time Instructor Belmont released them for dinner.

Knowing they'd trained the dogs hard all morning and part of the afternoon, Seven went to check on Goliath first. One of the interns was brushing him down.

"He doesn't mind that at all," Seven noted, pausing at the gate of the indoor cell. It was like a dog cage, but much bigger. Man-sized. The row of cages lined both walls of the kennel, and most of them were occupied.

"My name is India, in case you're wondering." The intern gestured at the dog with her brush. "He got away from me earlier and paid a visit to the kitchen. I'm working on our rapport to hopefully keep that from happening again."

"The kitchen, huh?" Seven wagged a finger at the dog. "Were you looking for a juicy bone?"

India shrugged. "He seemed more interested in visiting with the chef than anything else. I honestly don't recall her feeding him anything."

I was joking. The moment India mentioned

where Goliath had taken off to, Seven knew the dog must have been paying a visit to Tiffany. She was like his human mother. The two of them adored each other. Seven still had zero interest in negotiating a joint custody agreement with her. If his wife wanted a relationship so badly with his dog, then she could just suck it up and stay married to his owner.

That thought got him through his shower and dinner, a meal that was unsurprisingly filled with gushing commentary from Cecilia about their instructor.

Seven strolled alone to the parking lot after the meal was over, hoping to take a look at Tiff's faulty ignition. After circling the paved lot a few times, he had zero luck locating it. That was strange. Next, he hiked through the residential area that he'd over-heard several students and cadre members referring to as Instructor Row.

Most of the homes had recently undergone major renovations due to a vicious homeland terror attack that had taken place on this very street a few months ago. Some of them had been rebuilt from the foundation up.

Not sure which cabin Tiff lived in, he walked past them all, eyeing the vehicles in each driveway. Her car was nowhere in sight. Swallowing his disappointment, he dragged his tired limbs back to the men's dormitory to wait out the final minutes before East Whitlock's call. Nine o'clock rolled around, which was the start of Tiff's meeting time at the wedding shop. Then ten o'clock came and went. By the time eleven o'clock approached, Seven found himself fighting panic.

What was going on with Tiff? Was she safe? Had East made it in time to keep an eye on her? Assuming her meeting had only lasted an hour, she should be back on campus in another half hour or so. An hour tops.

Another fifteen minutes passed before Seven's phone finally buzzed with an incoming call.

He accepted the call and raised his cell phone to his ear. "Yeah?"

East jumped straight into his report. "I'm about to send you a whole slew of pictures."

"Is she alright?" Seven demanded anxiously.

"That depends on your definition of alright."

"So help me, East," he growled.

"She's headed back to the training center as we speak."

That was a relief. "And the bad news is…"

"Are you sitting down?"

Seven took a seat on the top stair of the second-story landing. "Yep."

"She's mixed up with a loan shark."

"You're kidding." His heart sank.

"Wish I was. Are you still sitting down?"

"Haven't moved." Seven was too exhausted to

move. He was beyond ready to face-plant into his bed and call it a night.

"Have my pictures come through yet?"

"No. Oh, wait. Here they come." Seven felt the buzz of several incoming text messages. "I'm going to take a quick look at them and be right back with you." He lowered his cell phone from his ear to scroll through East's snapshots. What he saw made his insides grow cold.

East had managed to get close enough to the shop to capture a photo of Tiff sitting across a table from a petite woman in a business suit. Her size was misleading, because she was on the FBI's most wanted list. Seven and his Texas Ranger comrades had jokingly referred to her in the past as The Megalodon.

She went under a whole list of pseudonyms. No one was a hundred percent certain of her legal name. Her criminal enterprise was that of a loan shark. However, she wasn't merely interested in collecting payments on exorbitantly high-interest loans. She always had a darker reason for why she chose her targets. And all too often, they ended up dead. She'd left a trail of bodies that stretched from the Atlantic to the Pacific.

"What does she want from my wife?" he demanded hoarsely.

"Money, for starters."

"What else?" He knew there had to be more to it.

And why did The Megalodon want money from his wife? Since he and Tiff had not taken out any loans during their marriage, he had to assume it was something she'd done before they tied the knot. *My lands, Tiff! Why didn't you say something to me?*

Had she seriously born this burden the entire time they'd been married? It was impossible to wrap his brain around that fact just yet. He was still absorbing it.

East was silent for so long that Seven wondered if he'd heard the question. Just as Seven was about to repeat it, he started speaking again. "I have a few contacts digging through databases as we speak. Only one thing has popped so far."

"Let's hear it."

"Two years ago you arrested a man suspected of being an associate of the Megalodon, though it was only proven a few days ago."

"Is he still behind bars?" If he was, he could be interrogated.

"In a manner of speaking. He was recently moved from solitary confinement on death row to a nearby psychiatric facility."

Meaning he likely wasn't in any condition to be interrogated. The psychiatric ward was where they transferred prisoners following a mental breakdown, which still didn't answer Seven's other burning question. "What's his association to the Megalodon?"

"Per the DNA comparison, he's her son."

Feeling like the wind had been knocked out of him, Seven tipped his head against the stair railing. This latest revelation cemented something in his mind. No matter what kind of debt Tiff had gotten embroiled in, she was innocent. She'd always been innocent.

"So, I'm the target," he muttered dully. A world-renowned fraudster had gone after his wife to get to him. The Megalodon would've carefully crafted her trap. Tiff had never seen it coming.

"Looks like."

Sickness coursed through Seven. It was a miracle his wife was still alive. The day she'd married him, she'd become the target of a heinous criminal. Heck, she'd probably been targeted the moment she started dating him. She'd been living, working, and going to college with an invisible set of crosshairs painted on her forehead.

"And you let her just get back on the road?" Seven choked, pushing to his feet. *In my truck, no less.* It was roughly equivalent to sending her down the highway in a rusty black metal coffin. A groan of self-recrimination tore through him. If he had any idea of the kind of danger she was heading into this evening, he would have never handed her his keys. On the contrary, he would have moved Heaven and Earth to prevent her from leaving town.

"If it makes you feel any better, she's inside an

armored vehicle. A federal agent is driving your truck."

No, it didn't make Seven feel any better. He gripped his head with both hands as fear for his wife's safety crashed over him. Never in all his years of serving as a Texas Ranger had he ever felt so helpless.

CHAPTER 7: DISTURBING GAME PLAN

SEVEN

No sooner did Seven end his call with East than a pair of uniformed employees converged on the stairwell.

One of them was Tiff's sous chef, of all people. Marcel Craft jogged up the stairs with a deadpan expression riding his dark features. "Officer Colburn, if you'll please come with us." Instead of giving a reason, he held up a badge. It was FBI, and not one of those fake ones that cosplay folks buy off the Internet, either. There was no mistaking the gold eagle and shield mounted against an oval backdrop of black leather.

On Marcel's heels was the other guy Seven had seen working in the kitchen with his wife. The wiry Hispanic fellow had also helped serve the continental breakfast that Seven and his classmates had enjoyed this morning. He joined Seven and

Marcel on the stair landing, flashing a second FBI badge.

Seven studied them through narrowed lids. Two federal agents working with his wife were no coincidence. It had to mean that she'd been under surveillance the entire time she'd been employed at the Texas Hotline Training Center.

He swiftly pocketed his cell phone.

The tall sous chef held out his hand. "I'm going to need to take a look at that."

Shaking his head, Seven reached back into his pocket to withdraw his spare phone. He always carried around two that looked identical to each other. One he used for his personal calls. The other he used for his business ones. It was a trick he'd learned while working undercover.

He slapped the spare phone against Marcel's palm a little harder than necessary. He could've made him wait until he produced a proper warrant for it, but it didn't feel worth the argument. For one thing, he was too tired. Secondly, he was outnumbered.

"Am I under arrest?" He'd never been big on small talk, always preferring to hear the bottom line first.

"What for?" A hint of humor danced through Marcel's dark, assessing gaze. "Did you commit a crime?" He gestured with both hands for Seven to walk down the stairs ahead of him.

"Not that I'm aware of." Seven got the distinct impression that the guy was enjoying his discomfort. As he moved down the stairs, he was surprised when no handcuffs were snapped onto his wrists. *Okay, so I'm not being arrested.* "Where are we going?"

"To the kitchen," Marcel's partner called in a cheerful voice from the landing. "Where else can a few hungry guys grab a bite to eat this late at night?"

If you say so. Seven felt more like tossing his cookies, but he didn't figure he had a choice in where they were heading. He stalked ahead of the two men across the grassy courtyard separating the men's dormitory from the building where the cafeteria and adjoining commercial kitchen were housed.

"Rear entrance," Marcel instructed in a low voice as he drew abreast of Seven.

When they reached the building, Marcel moved to unlock the door. Pushing it open, he stepped inside and flipped a switch.

Fluorescent light flooded the white and chrome kitchen, nearly blinding Seven. He held up an arm to shield his eyes until they had a chance to adjust to the light.

"In here." To Seven's surprise, Marcel made a beeline for Tiff's office.

When Seven joined him, he was grateful that the room was lit with nothing more than a desk light.

Marcel pointed at one of the two chairs in front of Tiff's desk. "Have a seat."

"I'll stand." Seven had no interest in getting with the FBI. He glanced around the office, hating all over again how sparse, empty, and un-Tiff-like it felt.

"Suit yourself." Marcel plopped into Tiff's chair and folded his arms. "You look ready to topple over."

Seven rounded on him. "How long have you had my wife under surveillance?"

"That's not how this works." Marcel's black eyebrows arched belligerently. "We'll be asking the questions."

Jamal pulled back one of the two chairs Seven had refused to sit in. "What my partner is trying to say is that Tiffany Colburn has been part of an ongoing federal investigation for the past year." He waved at the empty chair beside him. "Please join us. Our higher ups have instructed us to include you on our next play."

"Next play, huh?" Seven yanked the chair around to straddle it. "As far as I'm concerned, Tiff's safety isn't up for discussion. The moment she's back, I'm taking her off grid until this is over." His mind raced over their options and came up with one really good one — his grandfather's place. Skip Colburn had been living mostly off grid for years. He'd gone full-blown Texas Ranger when it came to security, though. The property was gated, and the farmhouse itself was fortified with steel doors, bullet-proof windows, and a safe room.

Marcel's head jerked. "Aren't you forgetting something?"

"Like what?"

"The fact that you and Tiffany are in the middle of a divorce, for one thing."

Seven gave him a hard look, surprised that he'd called it a divorce instead of a separation. "She'll come with me." He held the man's gaze, not bothering to hide his animosity. "Willingly." Or so he hoped.

"Are you sure that's wise?" Jamal half-rose from his chair to wedge himself between the two blustering men. He turned his head to meet Seven's gaze. "You're the target, Officer Colburn, so taking your wife anywhere right now won't get her out of danger."

"Anywhere with me, you mean." Seven scowled at him, unable to deny the facts he was laying out.

Marcel shrugged. "If the shoe fits."

Seven ignored him. "Are you saying it's better to leave her exposed here at the training center? From my angle, she's a sitting duck for whenever the Megalodon decides to take her next shot."

"I hear you, Officer Colburn, loud and clear," Jamal returned in a sympathetic voice. "I'm married, too, so I can only imagine what you're going through right now. To answer your question, though. Yes. It might be best to leave Tiffany at the training center for the time being, a proposition that I am happy to explain in as much detail as you'd like."

"He's married, not separated," Marcel interjected crisply, "in case you missed that part."

Seven wasn't sure what Marcel's problem was, though he had his suspicions. Before answering, he rocked his chair back on two legs to exhibit just how little effect the guy's gibes were having on him. He'd sat through dozens of interrogations and had conducted a good number of them himself, so he was very familiar with the games that were played to provoke a person into revealing more information.

"Here's an idea," he drawled. "If we're really on the same team, you might consider killing the good cop, bad cop routine. I have every reason to cooperate with you, since my wife's safety is at stake. Just lay your cards on the table so we can figure out the best way to make that happen."

"Are you saying you have the ability to look at your wife's situation with any level of objectivity?" Marcel scoffed, unwinding his arms to lean forward and steeple his hands on Tiff's desk. "Because I'm having a hard time swallowing that, considering the current status of your marriage."

Seven abruptly returned his chair to all four legs. "No one in their right mind expects the husband to be objective. I think the better question is, do *you* have the ability to remain objective while working alongside my wife, Agent Craft? If not, you might want to recuse yourself from the case."

There was a long stretch of silence in the room, during which Seven silently faced off with Marcel. They might as well have been two icebergs preparing to collide on a frigid ocean.

Without warning, Marcel's shoulders relaxed. He broke into a chuckle, shaking his head at Jamal while pointing at Seven. "I'm starting to like this guy."

Knowing the man's abrupt change in demeanor was intended to give him emotional whiplash, Seven snorted. "Give it time. The feeling will pass." He really didn't see any shared coffee breaks in their future.

Marcel spread his hands, swiveling Tiff's chair to face Seven again. "I'm sure you can understand my reservations about you." His smile disappeared as swiftly as it had appeared. "Your wife was targeted by a world renowned fraudster on your watch."

"I am aware." Seven ducked his head as a thousand volts of guilt shot straight through his heart.

"Instead of picking up on the clues, you let it destroy your marriage."

Not entirely! Seven yanked his head up, not yet willing to abandon all hope in that direction. "Apparently there's some truth to the old proverb that love is blind, Agent Craft. Despite my many failures as a husband, however, Tiff and I are very much still married, something you seem to have a difficult time accepting. Why?" In his experience, the quickest way to stay alive in a fight was to throw the next punch.

"So, you still love her," Marcel mused, eyeing him slyly. It wasn't worded as a question, and he didn't seem to expect a response. He cocked his head at Jamal with a flourishing wave in Seven's direction. "He's all yours."

Though Seven was exhausted, he deduced that Marcel was finished psycho-analyzing him and his struggling marriage. For now, anyway.

"Here's the deal." Jamal started talking rapidly, which Seven had no doubt was to keep him off balance. "Tiffany was followed by a team of federal agents to Houston tonight. The wedding shop where she met with the Megalodon was bugged with recording devices in advance. Although our team is still studying the feeds, the preliminary conclusion is this. Your wife has managed to establish a measure of rapport with our target, and—"

"Whoa!" Seven stopped him right there with an upraised hand. "You're saying you had the Mega-lodon in your sights, and you just let her go?"

"Tonight's meeting sounded a lot like a reunion between a former bride and her wedding planner. And evidence gathered was circumstantial, at best." Marcel held up a finger as if instructing a small child. "Our deadly fraudster has done a very good job of covering her tracks. Identifying her son was the first time we were able to link any forensics at all to her. We're closing in, but we need more evidence to build a case."

"During which time you intend to use my wife as bait." Raw fury sliced through Seven, beating back his exhaustion. He stood to signify that he was done negotiating.

"I wouldn't use the word bait, per se," Jamal hastened to say. "What we're hoping to work out with you and your wife is more of a partnership. You want this fraudster behind bars as badly as we do, preferably before she racks up any more casualties. More importantly, you want a future for your wife that doesn't entail her spending the rest of her life looking over her shoulder."

"What would this partnership look like?" Bait was bait, no matter what they chose to call it. Over Seven's dead body were they using Tiff as such.

Jamal leaned forward in his chair. "It would look the same as it did when you woke up this morning. You'll still be a Texas Ranger immersed in a month of elite search and rescue training. Tiffany will still be our lovely head chef, preparing three square meals per day for a famished student body."

"What's the catch?" Seven was waiting for the other shoe to drop. He knew how these arrangements worked. There was always a catch.

"Tiffany will stay in contact with the Megalodon, who worked out a little side deal of her own with your wife last night."

"What side deal?" Seven's apprehension increased several notches.

"Well, last night was supposed to be Tiff's final payment to close out the financing agreement for her wedding dress."

"Her wedding dress? You're telling me that's how that witch got her hooks into my wife?" *By financing her blasted wedding dress?* Seven shook his head, having a difficult time believing Tiff would have fallen for something so foolish. In the entire year they were married, he'd watched her clip coupons and stretch a dollar farther than anyone else he'd ever known. She was the definition of frugal.

"Yeah." Marcel's voice was sarcastic. "Her wedding. Because it's only the most important day in a woman's life. You know, when she's trying to impress the most important man in her life."

Seven ignored his sarcasm, refusing to let the guy get under his skin. "I was already impressed with her. Already hers." *Heart and soul.* How could she not have known that?

Jamal spread his hands, his wide mouth twisting in a grimace. "Whatever the reasons, Tiffany accepted a loan from the Megalodon, who doesn't seem inclined to let her off the hook just yet."

"What has she strong-armed my wife into this time?" Seven braced himself for more bad news. If there was another deal in play with the Megalodon, the fight was far from over.

"For starters, she refused the final payment for the wedding dress."

Uh-oh. "In exchange for—?"

"Well, that's where things get tricky." Jamal watched him closely. "Apparently, the Megalodon got wind of your legal separation, which Tiffany had previously indicated to her would be a divorce. It appears that the Megalodon cancelled the balance of Tiffany's loan for the express purpose of funding your big D. In exchange for her generosity —"

"Generosity?" Seven choked. The Megalodon was a dangerous criminal who did nothing out of benevolence. The fact that she didn't mind adding his and Tiff's marriage to her growing pile of collateral damage was proof that her heart was as black as the hinges on the gates of hell.

"In her twisted mind, she is being generous. In exchange, she wishes for Tiffany to spy on you during your stint at the training center."

Criminies! "So, she knows where my wife works." That was news to Seven. He lifted his hat to drag a hand through his hair, mentally reverting to his original plan to snatch his wife and run the next time he laid eyes on her.

Muted voices outside her office alerted him to the fact that the kitchen was receiving more visitors this evening. He glanced in irritation at the door, wondering who else was wandering around campus at this hour instead of getting some much needed sleep.

"Considering that you're the Megalodon's real target, Officer Colburn, our greater concern is that she knows your location for the next month. Not to worry, though. We already have a team embedded here, and we'll be keeping close tabs on the situation. Tiffany will be guarded and coached every step of the way."

Seven had no doubt that Marcel was going to enjoy the "coaching" part more than he should. "I want round-the-clock security on her," he growled.

"Done." Marcel stood. "In return, we need your cooperation in finalizing your divorce so the indeterminate state of your marriage doesn't blow the cover on our whole operation."

"Wait! What?" Seven glared at the two federal agents. Maybe he was more tired than he realized, because he truly hadn't seen this one coming. Divorcing his wife wasn't his idea of cooperating with an investigation. Far from it! They couldn't be serious.

At their grave expressions, he fiercely shook his head. *Okay, so you are serious.* "The answer is no." What they were asking for was unconscionable. He was fast losing patience with them. "If you don't have a better offer, this conversation is over. Under no circumstances am I giving up on my marriage."

"I'm sorry, Seven," his wife's voice wafted across the room from the doorway, "but I've already signed the divorce paperwork."

He spun around to face her, relieved to see her alive and well, though aghast at her words. "Tiff!" His voice gave a suspicious crack. "You can't do this." *Please don't do this.*

She was wearing her favorite black jumpsuit, a color she claimed was slimming. Not that he'd ever cared about stuff like that. Her blonde hair was pulled back in a simple but elegant twist. Silver hoops dangled from her ears. As usual, she never failed to take his breath away. At the moment, it felt more like suffocating.

He found himself wishing he was in something besides his faded jeans and scuffed boots. He wished his hands were less callused and his vocabulary more refined. She deserved a better man than him in her life. However, she'd chosen him once upon a time, and he wasn't letting her go without a fight.

His gaze dropped to the paperwork in her hand, and then it hit him. The feds had already "coached" her into serving him with the divorce paperwork, probably because she was the one person in the world they knew he wouldn't say no to.

The color seeped from her face as she extended it to him. "She's a very dangerous woman, Seven. If this is the only way for us to get her..."

He shook his head helplessly. "There has to be

another way." As he took a staggering step toward her, he was dimly aware of Marcel and Jamal quietly making their exit.

Tiffany flinched as the door clicked shut behind them. "I'm so sorry, Seven," she repeated softly. "For everything. I know you want answers from me, but I don't know where to even begin." She swayed on her feet.

For one heart-shaking moment, he feared she was about to faint. He sprang in her direction, reaching her in the nick of time. She slumped forward into his arms.

CHAPTER 8: KEEPING UP APPEARANCES

TIFFANY

The divorce papers slipped from Tiffany's hand as Seven's arms came around her. She clung to him, burying her face against his chest. "I'm so sorry, Seven." She knew she was babbling, but the time for silence was past. By now, he probably knew every sordid detail about her miserable part in the whole financial fraud scheme. The FBI was involved. She'd be lucky if she and Seven got out of this alive.

"Me, too," he whispered hoarsely. Instead of the anger she expected from him, he pressed his lips to the top of her head. "I don't know how I could've been so blind. I should have known something else was going on."

Her blood chilled at the realization that the man she'd married loved her so much that he was ready to forgive her right here and now. However, now wasn't the time for kissing and making up. Not yet. Most unfortunately, she was going to have to test the extent of his loyalties a little longer.

"It's okay, sugar." She raised her damp face to meet his gaze. "Heaven knows we aren't the first couple who tried and failed." The only other time she'd called him sugar, he'd teased her mercilessly about it. Apparently, some weirdo crush from high school had called him that a few times. He'd hated the term ever since. The only reason she was using the term now was to put him on alert. She silently prayed that he would catch on quickly and play along.

Seven grew deathly still. Then he loosened his grasp on her and leaned back to study her with his eyes blazing blue fire. "How can you say that?" he demanded harshly.

"Because it's true. We both know it is." She reached behind her to lower his arm from her waist. Before she let it go, she slid her fingers down his arm to press a message into his palm. Before she'd walked into her office, she'd managed to scribble a few words on a piece of masking tape.

Though his accusing gaze continued to burn into hers, the way his hand briefly clasped hers told her that he understood she was trying to send him a message.

She had no doubt there were hidden cameras in her office, recording every nuance of her confrontation with him. Surely, he suspected that, as well.

That was why they couldn't risk speaking openly to each other. Not yet. For the life of her, she had no idea who she could trust anymore. Except Seven, of course. Even when she'd been the angriest with him, she'd never stopped trusting him.

"So that's it?" He abruptly jerked away from her and started pacing her office, jamming his hands in the pockets of his jeans. "You're just going to quit on us?"

She stared after him with bated breath, willing him to sneak a peek at the message she'd taped to his hand. "The important thing is, we tried to make it work, didn't we? We'll always have that to hang on to."

When he swung back in her direction, his expression was so livid that her heart sank. "It was one measly year of marriage, Tiff." He viciously stabbed the air with his finger. "In my book, that's not trying very hard. But if it makes you feel any better to lie to yourself, be my guest." He held his hands up, palms facing her in a gesture that indicated he was washing his hands of the whole situation. "I'm sick to death of arguing with you. I'm tired all the way to my soul of being the only one fighting for our marriage."

Her eyes moved to the hand where she'd left her message. The tape was gone from his palm. Her message had been all the more desperate for its shortness and simplicity. She'd written: *Make it look real*.

Holy breakfast muffins, but he was doing that and then some! Tears of relief stung the backs of Tiffany's eyelids. She briefly closed her eyes at the realization that her husband had not only read her message, but that he was doing what she'd asked without question. She didn't have to fake the sobs clawing their way up her throat as she opened her eyelids and met his gaze again. "That's not true. The fact that you would even make such a claim only underscores how broken our relationship is. Like my mother always said, it takes two people to make a marriage work, and it takes two people to break it apart."

Her mother hadn't said anything of the sort, and Seven knew it. All she'd done was predict gloom and doom for their future together, since they'd taunted fate by getting married on Friday the thirteenth. Her words, not theirs. Ros Becker had more superstitions than a centipede had legs.

Seven curled his upper lip as he advanced on her. "Oh, now you want to bring your mother into things? The same woman who's never had a kind word to spare anyone, much less her only son-in-law?" His voice grew so harsh that Tiffany did a double take. It was getting harder to tell how much of their latest argument was real as opposed to how much was playacting.

"That's not fair." His venom made her catch her breath. "This hasn't been easy on her, either, you know. Watching her only child marry a man who's gone all the time."

"There you go again." Seven shook his head at her. "Blaming me for stuff out of my control. Despising me for simply doing my job. After a while, it gets old being the bad guy all the time, Tiff. Really old."

"See?" She pointed at him, giving him her best *aha* look through her tears. "That's what I'm talking about. You sound like a man who gave up on our marriage a long time ago." She twisted around to stoop and pick up the divorce paperwork she'd dropped earlier. "Just admit it, and sign the papers already." She waved them impatiently at him.

After another scraping, head-to-toe look, he snatched them from her. Stalking to her desk, he reached for a pen, knocking her pen holder over in the process.

While the ink pens and Number #2 lead pencils scattered like skewer sticks across her desk, she silently prayed that her husband would notice the other clues she'd left him. Though her middle name was Rosalea and her married surname was a hyphenated version of her maiden name and his last name, she'd signed her name as *Tiffany Rose Colburn.* She'd purposefully misspelled her middle name and left off the first half of her last name. If the clerks at the county registrar's office were doing their jobs, there was no way they'd process paperwork without first kicking it back for corrections.

It was a flimsy trick that would hopefully go unnoticed by the FBI and therefore buy her and Seven a little more time. Divorcing him was the last thing she wanted. Though their passionate confrontation during the past few minutes would hopefully indicate otherwise on the hidden surveillance cameras, she was still fighting for their marriage. She would fight for it until she drew her last breath.

Seven's scrawling signature on the divorce papers was barely legible, but he'd somehow managed to make the first two letters of his last name look more like "No" than "Co." Gosh, but it was so Seven of him! She almost laughed out loud.

His features were set in such cold, hard lines when he turned to face her again that she shivered in apprehension. The fact that he was playing along with her ruse in no way meant things were okay between them.

"So, this is it." He handed the divorce papers back to her. "No more acting required, huh? We'll go back to pretending like we don't know each other in public. Shoot!" His voice rang with sarcasm. "It'll almost make it feel like we're still married."

She wrinkled her nose in derision as she accepted the paperwork from him. "Just because we're divorced doesn't mean we can't be civil to each other." Quickly flipping through the pages, she noted how he'd left the same section blank that she had where their initials were supposed to be affixed. If anyone cut a corner and initialed the blanks for her and Seven, the forgeries would be further reason down the road to declare their divorce null and void.

"Civil?" he sneered. "You walk out on our marriage, take off with our life savings, and hand me a divorce. But Heaven forbid I say or do anything that you consider to be uncivil."

"Oh, my gosh! Really? All you ever do is harp about money. I'm not going to miss it." She dug in her purse and yanked out the white envelope full of cash. "Here." She thrust it at him. "Maybe this will stop your griping."

He opened the flap and thumbed through the money. "This is more than what you owe me." The look he shot her held a note of genuine curiosity. He was waiting for some indication as to what she wanted him to do with the funds.

"Take it before I change my mind," she snapped. "This makes us even. I seriously don't want to hear another word about my college tuition." The enve-lope included every penny she'd received from the sale of her car and wedding ring. It would be safer in his possession than hers.

"Nothing can pay me back for everything you put me through." He pocketed the envelope, shaking his head. "Probably took years off my life."

"Seven!" Pretending to be perplexed, she stared at him as he stalked to the door. "I'm not the enemy here. In case you've forgotten, she's back in Houston plotting your downfall."

He made a sound of disgust as he yanked open the door. "Well, we sure as heck aren't friends, Tiff."

Marcel was the first one to pop his head inside the door of her office after Seven left. "Is the coast clear?"

She held up a hand. "I'm not in the mood to talk about it." She remained behind her desk, willing her insides to stop trembling.

"Understood." His dark gaze landed on the divorce papers stacked neatly on her desk. He pointed at them. "How about I get those out of your way so you don't have to look at them anymore?"

She waved him forward. "Thanks." It was the only syllable she could squeak out without breaking down altogether in front of him.

He silently moved into the room to retrieve the paperwork, then just as silently returned to the doorway with it. With one last worried glance at her, he left her alone with her thoughts.

Once he disappeared around the corner, she collapsed in her chair and dropped her head on her desk. She'd done all she could. The rest was up to her husband.

He'd handled their encounter tonight so much better than she'd expected, making her realize just how badly she'd underestimated the man she'd married. At the moment, all she could do was regret every snarky comment she'd ever made about his work schedule. She was overcome with remorse about all the times she'd been angry at him for being late for dinner, missing the outings she'd planned, and being absent from his side of the bed when she rolled over at night.

Seven might not have been there every time she wanted him to be, but his loyalty to her had never faltered. He was strong, clever, and brave. And despite the exhaustion lines around the edges of his eyes this evening, his Texas Ranger instincts had been firing on all pistons. He'd been able to act on his feet, to adapt and improvise his behavior as she'd frantically fed him information about the trouble she was in.

And in doing so, he'd managed to make her fall in love with him all over again. *You're my hero, Seven!* She allowed herself the luxury of reliving the magic of being in his arms again. To feel the brush of his hard mouth against the top of her head one more time. He was the only person in the world who'd ever made her feel so adored and cherished.

Being with him had also given her hope again — hope that they might actually stand a shot at defeating the Megalodon. The events of this evening had forced her to give up the notion that she could handle the situation alone. She'd been the world's biggest fool for ever thinking she could.

Despite her mother's mumbo jumbo about how unlucky it was to have married on Friday the thirteenth, Tiffany knew better. Becoming Texas Ranger Seven Colburn's wife was seriously the best decision she'd ever made. She hoped she lived long enough to tell him.

SEVEN STORMED from his wife's office, keeping his head down and his expression livid for the sake of anyone who was watching. For reasons he didn't fully understand, Tiff was begging him to make their split look real. It must mean she didn't trust everyone around her right now. Anyone but her own husband, that is, which meant even the smug-faced Agent Craft was outside her inner circle of trust.

He replayed her message in his head. *Make it look real.* Within the simplicity of those four short words, he felt like he'd recovered the woman he was afraid he'd lost forever. Despite all her fear he sensed lurking beneath the surface, Tiff was still fighting for their marriage. She'd never stopped. The way she'd signed their divorce papers proved it. It made his heart sing and gave him the strength to do what needed to be done next.

His exhaustion from earlier was long gone. In its

place was a renewed determination to defend and protect the woman he'd never stopped loving. *I'll get you out of this, darling. Just hang in there a little longer.* She was in a precarious position, no lie. They both were. But now that he had some idea of what they were up against, he could form a plan to extricate them.

Jamal jogged up to Seven as he reached the rear exit. "So, uh, it's business as usual, okay? Keep training. Keep up appearances. Just keep on keeping on."

The fact that Jamal considered divorce paperwork to be business as usual was a real head shaker. Seven paused at the door, tempted to set him straight on a few things. However, he held back. If Tiff didn't fully trust the guy, he shouldn't either. After a pause, he merely grated out the words, "Roger that." He turned the doorknob. "Anything else?"

For an answer, Jamal held out the phone that Marcel had insisted on taking a look at. "I added Marcel and me to your contacts. Plus, you know where to find us if you need anything." He waved at the room. "I'll be on kitchen duty. It's hard to contain my excitement, but I'll manage. Somehow."

"Yep." Unable to scrape up a smile at the guy's attempt at humor, Seven accepted the phone and stuffed it in his pocket. Because of what was at stake, he had to assume the FBI had added a tracking device to it. He wouldn't be surprised if they were tapping his line as well. He'd have to keep that in mind with every step he took and every call he made going forward. Fortunately, he knew just the guy to help him reverse engineer what they'd done, if need be.

Reaching the men's dormitory, Seven stealthily slid his boots from his feet and crawled beneath the covers of his lower bunk bed. Pulling them over his head, he unstrapped the cell phone Marcel and Jamal didn't know about from his chest holster and shot off his first encrypted message to East.

Fake divorce in process. Tiff wants our split to look real. Must be a mole.

East would know he was referring to the feds. His response came seconds later. *Help on the way. In place by morning.*

Knowing there was nothing more productive he could do besides get some sleep, Seven returned the secure phone to his chest holster, rolled to his side, and closed his eyes.

It seemed like only minutes later that he awoke. A quick glance at his watch revealed it was ten minutes before his alarm went off. He sat up in bed with gritty eyes and the start of a headache. *Nice.* Swinging his legs to the floor, he moved to the foot of his bed to rummage through the storage trunk resting there. He retrieved his bottle of Tylenol and popped a few pills into his mouth. Then he headed to the men's room with a change of clothing draped over his shoulder and his toiletry bag tucked beneath an arm.

A few guys were already showering. Seven could hear the spray of water and see the steam rising above their curtained stalls. He quickly dumped his toiletry bag on the sink and pulled out his razor. A lot of his classmates had joked about not shaving the whole month they were there. Normally Seven might have done the same thing, but Tiff was on site and Tiff had always preferred a smooth, clean shave.

"Would you like another towel, sir?"

The unexpectedly familiar voice was a jolt to Seven's senses. However, he forced himself to finish rinsing his face and patting it dry before glancing over his shoulder.

Good gravy! East Whitlock hadn't been kidding about sending help or having it in place by morning. To be more specific, he'd sent himself.

The sight of his friend in a green cleaning staff uniform was a truly welcome one. The former Texas Ranger had donned a shaggy silver wig and beard and was stooped over a roller cart overflowing with supplies. There were paper towels and disinfectant spray bottles on the top shelf and refill soap and clean linens on the bottom shelf. On one side of the cart was a set of rubber clasps, holding up a collection of brooms and mops. Mounted to the end of the cart was a double canvas bin for soiled linen and refuse. A logo for the Bloom Where You're Planted Cleaning Service was emblazoned across the canvas bin — cheerful pink, orange, and yellow flowers with smiling faces.

Seven committed every detail to his photo-graphic memory with a single glance. "Thanks." Keeping his voice carefully offhand, he spun around to accept the towel with both hands. There was no telling what East was hiding within its folds. Sure enough, he could feel the shape of something hard. He sauntered deeper into the men's room to claim one of the empty shower stalls. The moment the curtain was shut behind him, he unrolled the towel and found a small burner phone resting there.

Flipping it open, he read the message East had typed on the screen. *It's for her*. A quick check proved that both his private line and East's had been pre-programmed in. This was good. Now they would have a secure way of communicating — after he delivered the phone to her, of course.

As he showered and changed, he mentally rehearsed a few different scenarios for how to make that happen. Each of them came with their own set of risks, some better than others. However, he knew it wouldn't come down to his personal preference. He would simply have to take the first opportunity that presented itself.

Like the other new recruits, he didn't take his time strolling to the Cafeteria. He jogged. There was no rule about trainees having to hustle, but every part of their day had been rigidly scheduled. If they were late for breakfast, they'd miss out on eating.

Once inside the door, he joined the lengthy line of students waiting for food. When he reached the front of the line, he picked up a clean tray, plate, and set of silverware. Both Marcel and Jamal were helping Tiff serve breakfast again this morning.

There was no sign of recognition in Marcel's features when Seven reached him. It seemed to Seven that he went out of his way to slop the serving of eggs and grits all over the place, though. When he was finished scooping, cheese was stringing down the side of the plate. He handed it to Jamal, who placed a few strips of bacon on it. Tiff was the last employee in the serving line. She added a biscuit to the edge of Seven's plate and handed it back with a strained expression.

For a moment, it appeared she intended to keep her face averted as he accepted the plate from her. However, at the last second, she flicked a nervous glance at him. It was long enough for him to angle his head toward the end of the line, urging her to follow his lead. "Think I heard someone complaining the ketchup was out." He infused a bit of sarcasm into his voice. "You might be getting another complaint if I get down there and find out it's true."

She rolled her eyes in Jamal and Marcel's direction, giving Seven his second stab of apprehension. If she assigned one of them the honors of handling the refill, it would defeat the purpose. "Just for the record, I'm refilling the ketchup under protest. I've never understood why anyone would punish eggs like that."

Marcel made some rejoinder about unrefined palates. "But what do I know?" He snickered. "All I did was go to chef school."

His description struck Seven as a little odd. He'd been expecting the sous chef to say culinary school. Nobody called it chef school. *What a weirdo!* He tucked the detail away in his head for future reference.

Seven matched his stride to Tiff's as she marched in high dudgeon toward the condiments bar. He watched out of the corner of his eye as she rounded the end of the serving line to make her way around to the ketchup dispenser, at which point he deliberately plowed in to her. His plate of food went skidding off his tray and splashed against the front of her white jacket.

While she was busy yelping with surprise, he slid the burner phone into one of her pockets. They sprang back from each other, and she watched in dismay as the contents of his tray finished crashing to the floor. The white porcelain plate shattered in all directions.

He bent over to clean it up, tickled to death that he'd accomplished his mission so easily. After a moment of hesitation, Tiff stooped over to help out, muttering something beneath her breath about how he'd better hurry up and get back in line before he starved to death.

In response, he cocked his head at her and lifted the biscuit to his mouth that he'd been careful to grab before the rest of his food went flying. With a belligerent jut of his chin, he took a bite, chewed, and swallowed it while she watched.

"Thanks for the ketchup," he sneered. Then he stood and walked away, leaving her to clean up the mess alone.

The next several days were long and grueling, and Seven had the added pressure of being embroiled in a federal criminal case. It made the constant complaining of a few of his classmates particularly annoying.

"I never thought I would hate my life this much," the redheaded Cecilia sighed as they returned their dogs to the kennel Saturday evening. "This is ten times worse than the police academy was."

Throughout the past week, he'd learned she'd recently been transferred to a search and rescue unit in Austin. She'd dropped a few hints to him about making the move from San Antonio for a fresh start following a bad breakup. Though it was clear she was burning to talk about her ex-boyfriend, he didn't ask any questions because he didn't want to get involved. Despite his efforts to avoid her, she was constantly glued to his side.

After trotting her perky little Boston terrier alongside his Doberman on their way to the kennel, she sought him out again in the cafeteria. Sliding her tray onto the table, she plopped into the seat directly to his right.

He debated ignoring her, but a flash of purple made him cast a sideways glance in her direction. His eyes nearly bugged out. Though he quickly returned his attention to his plate, the image of her hip-hugging jean cutoffs and swooping purple halter top remained seared in his mind.

Wow! Not exactly the typical wardrobe of a search and rescue student, but okay.

"Seriously, Seven, I'm about to lose it. I came here to be molded into a razor sharp search and rescuer, not to eat sub-par food and have to hunt down my own soap for the bathroom sink."

"It's steak." He pointed with his knife at the sizable hunk of meat squatting in the center of her plate.

"There's a fly swimming in the gravy," she returned glumly.

Overcome with curiosity, he leaned closer. Sure enough, there was a two-winged insect half submerged in the milk gravy. He straightened with a chuckle. "Looks like yours came with a little extra protein."

"How can you joke about stuff like this?" She wrinkled her freckled nose at him. "Flies carry like a million diseases around with them." She shoved her tray away, her red-painted lips twisted into a pout.

"That many?" he pretended surprise. "I had no idea."

"Gosh! You're such a jerk!" She lifted her soda glass and took a slurp of it through her straw.

Shaking his head, he went back to eating. It wasn't like he'd sought out her company, and he certainly wasn't seeking her approval.

"Aw! Did I hurt your feelings?" she cooed, setting her glass down. Without warning, she threw her arms around his middle. "I was just kidding." She batted her mascara-drenched lashes up at him. "Sort of."

To his intense irritation, when she lifted her head from his shoulder, one of her hands slid across the holster strapped beneath his shirt.

It was in that moment that his first suspicions about her bloomed into existence. At a training institute that was crawling with federal agents and heaven only knew what else, who was to say that the Megalodon hadn't managed to plant one of her own goons in his very squad? It was only a theory, but it made an odd sort of sense. Why else would any woman continue to shower him with so much attention after he'd made it clear to her he wasn't interested?

He might be wrong about Cecilia, but her background would bear looking into — just in case. With Tiff's safety at stake, he wasn't leaving any stone unturned. Later this evening, he'd ask East to do a little digging in her direction.

He reached up to lower Cecilia's slender hand from his chest. "Actually, you were point on about me being a jerk." He meant it as a warning.

She merely giggled and cocked her head at him. As she eyed him, her expression sobered. "Listen, Seven, I'm sorry if your ex made you feel that way, but it isn't true."

Another alarm bell went off in his head. "I don't recall saying anything about my relationship status."

She made a face at him. "You didn't have to. It's written all over your sour attitude towards women in general. Plus, I'm pretty sure there's an indentation on your finger where a wedding ring used to be."

He wiggled his fingers beneath her nose so she could get a better look at it. "It's a scar." Because of his job, he didn't wear his wedding ring very often, certainly not often enough to leave an indentation. The mark Cecilia was referring to was from an old injury. His hand had gotten caught on a latch in his grandfather's barn years ago. The rusty old hardware had taken a piece of his skin with it.

She reached up to lace her fingers through his. "Then what's your story, Officer Colburn? Are you single and looking, or hitched to the old ball and chain?"

"Not looking." He disengaged his hand from hers, wondering if she was capable of taking a hint.

"That's not an answer."

"Actually, it is." Since she clearly wasn't going to let up on him anytime soon, he stabbed his fork through the remaining section of his steak and stood with the tray in his other hand. "See you in the morning." He abruptly left the table, polishing off the rest of his steak as he walked toward the tray drop-off area.

The phone strapped to his chest buzzed with an incoming message. He took a quick detour into the men's room and found an empty stall. Latching the door behind him, he withdrew the phone to read the message. It was from East.

Rendezvous in the Human Resources Department. Wait for the official call.

His regular phone rang before he left the stall. He lifted the phone to his ear. "Officer Colburn speaking."

"Hey! This is your friendly Human Resources clerk. We need you to stop by the main office to fill out one more form for your scholarship. We must have overlooked it on your first day. I'm really sorry about the inconvenience."

"That's alright. I can head there now, if that works for you."

"I was really hoping you'd say that." She sounded relieved. Then her voice became muffled, as if she was cupping her hand around the phone. "Actually, the scholarship rep is here in the office right now, breathing down my neck about it."

He chuckled, figuring she was referring to East. "On my way."

In case Cecilia was still lurking, he looked both ways before exiting the men's room. The coast was clear. He took a side exit from the building and headed straight for the main office.

He found the Human Resources clerk looking harried with her corkscrew salt-and-pepper curls flying in all directions. "There you are," she exclaimed, pushing her reading glasses higher on her nose. She pointed at one of the conference room doors. "Please forgive me for passing the buck, but that scholarship rep I was telling you about is still here. If you'll just meet with him real quick and knock out that form for us..."

"Happy to." He gave her a mock salute and moved across the reception area to enter the conference room.

As expected, he found East Whitlock on the other side. This time, he was wearing a serious-looking navy business suit with a pinstripe shirt and red power tie.

Seven snorted as he leaned in to slap him on the

back. "If your day job doesn't work out, you were made for the stage, bro."

The answering chuckle to his words was distinctly female. And wildly familiar. Seven's heart wrenched with longing as he stepped back from East and swung around to face his wife.

As a precaution, he mechanically divested himself of all electronic devices, handing them blindly to his friend.

"You're welcome." East pocketed the phones and punched him lightly in the shoulder before making himself scarce.

Seven wasn't sure if he'd moved into the adjoining conference chamber or stepped into the storage closet, nor did he care. Finding himself unexpectedly alone with his wife was the best gift anyone could've possibly given him.

They stared at each other for a long moment. Like him, she'd showered and changed out of her work uniform. She had on a pair of faded denim capris that accentuated her mouth-watering curves and a pink sleeveless top cascading with lacy ruffles. Her blonde hair was swinging halfway down her back, just begging for him to run his fingers through it.

However, this was her game. He watched longingly, waiting for her to make her next move.

"Seven." Her voice came out husky with emotion as she sashayed shyly in his direction. "I've rehearsed what I was going to say to you at least a thousand times in my head." Her smile was sad. "I just wasn't sure I was ever going to get a chance to say any of it." She reached him and paused in front of him. "And now that you're here in the same room with me, none of the words I prepared seem adequate."

He balled his hands into fists at his sides to keep from reaching for her. "I don't need a speech, Tiff." All he needed was a sign — any indication at all from the woman who was fighting so hard to stay married to him — that he still had the right to take her in his arms.

"Okay." She nervously bit her lower lip. "Here goes. I've made a lot of mistakes in my life. Too many. But marrying you was not one of them."

The green light Seven had been waiting for flashed brightly in his mind's eye, nearly blinding him. His arms encircled her so quickly that she gasped in surprise.

"Seven," she sighed, sliding her arms around his neck as his lips descended on hers.

He brushed his mouth against hers once, twice, sampling instead of devouring, giving them both a chance to relearn the feel of each other.

"I love you," she whispered brokenly against his lips, "so very much."

Her words burned through him like wildfire, eating away months of angst and loneliness. So much for his intention to take things slow with her! He yanked her closer, slanting his mouth hungrily over hers and taking them deeper — much deeper, to the place they both wanted to go.

She kissed him back, giving as much as she took, leaving him with no doubt that she still belonged to him

She pulled back before he was even close to finished kissing her. "I have so much to tell you, baby, but we don't have much time."

He gazed into her shining blue eyes and found the same storm of emotions churning there that were churning inside of him. "As much as I love you, Tiff, I'd be lying if I didn't say your best bet right now is to take our divorce papers and run as far from me as possible."

"Really?" She dragged her hand through his hair, pulling his head close again so she could rest her forehead against his. "Because that's not happening."

Buoyed by the fierceness of her tone, he kissed his way down her cheek and pressed his face to the side of her neck. "I'm the reason you're in this mess, Tiff. They came after you to get to me. You understand that, right?"

"I didn't when it started," she confessed in a shaky voice, "but I do now." She trailed her fingers up his rough jawline to trace the shape of his ear. "And I have to tell you, it makes all my previous frustrations about our relationship seem really small and petty. I spent our first year of marriage fretting way too much over how many times you were late to dinner and other stupid stuff like that. I had no real appreciation for the dangers you were facing every day. No idea how precious every moment was with you, even when you were too tired to do anything but hold me as you fell asleep. Well, I get it now."

He smiled against her neck. "If you truly got it, darling, you'd take off running." He hugged her tighter to let her know that was the last thing he wanted.

"I'm right where I want to be, Seven." He could feel the dampness of tears on his chin. "As long as you're willing to take me back when this is all over."

He snorted. "Just so you know, I already tore up my copy of the separation agreement."

Her whole body shook as her sobs grew stronger. "I, um...there's something else I need to tell you. At first, I wasn't going to, because I was too busy blaming you for everything, but I've learned my lesson. Keeping secrets from you is never a good thing. I should have told you the moment it happened."

For a moment, his insides went cold, thinking she was about to confess she'd cheated on him. He could see how it might've happened, too. Like she said, he'd been gone way too much, and he'd been too tired to love her the way she deserved half the time when he was home.

"It'll probably help you understand why I went

off the deep end and filed for that awful separation in the first place," she sighed. "It's taken me months to pull myself back together, but after I lost the baby, I sort of fell apart for a while."

He went still. *Baby? What baby?* He abruptly lifted his head to take in her tear-ravaged face. It wasn't the expression of a woman confessing that she'd been unfaithful to him. It was the shattered look of someone who'd suffered something far more excruciating.

She'd been pregnant at some point, and now she wasn't.

He frowned in confusion as the first fissures of sadness speared their way through him. "Why didn't you tell me you were pregnant?"

"I wanted to," she rasped. "I was planning to right after the doctor confirmed it. He said I was about six weeks along." She closed her eyes as if the memories were too painful to repeat. "I bought a new daddy greeting card for you and baked a cake, but you never made it home. It was the night of that hostage situation down at the convenience store. You were gone for three days and three nights. Then, after your sergeant called to let me know you'd gone in for the hostage and hadn't come out at the agreed upon time, I, er..." She stopped talking, and more tears dripped down her cheeks.

Seven's heart felt like it was dropping to the floor. "You miscarried."

"Yes." She wrapped her arms around his neck again and held on tightly. "It happened a few hours before you made it home. And even though the doctor swore it was just one of those things that happens when a woman's body isn't ready to bear a child, I blamed your job. I blamed you." She sniffed damply. "I was wrong. I thought nothing in the world would ever compare to the pain of losing our baby. However, the kind of pain I've experienced in the past month at the thought of losing you..." She shuddered. "It's never going to fade, Seven. If I lose you, I won't survive it."

By the time she finished sharing her heartache with him, his face was as damp as hers. He wished he could come up with an eloquent response, but fancy words had never been his strength. Instead, he reached up to fist a hand in her hair and gently tip her face up to his. "The only way you're going to lose me, Tiff, is if you tell me to go."

"I don't want you to."

"You'd be safer a few thousand miles away from me, darling. That's the truth."

"I'd much rather take my chances together. I mean it, Seven." Her lashes fluttered against her cheeks a few times, leaving more damp streaks. "I'm sorry it took me so long to figure it out, but I think this is the for better or worse part of our vows. I think being married means more than just being happy together. We're also supposed to be sad together, afraid together, and whatever else we have to deal with...together."

"Yep." He touched his mouth to hers again. "You're the best part of my life, Tiff, on both the good days and the bad days."

She smiled through her tears. "Even though I'll never get tired of making messes in the kitchen and will always pack a few extra pounds?"

He couldn't believe she felt the need to ask him something so ridiculous after everything they'd been through. "Really, Tiff?" He shook his head at her. "If you haven't figured out by now that you're perfect just the way you are, then I really need to step up my game." He playfully dipped her over his arm and took her under for another soul-shaking kiss.

She came up laughing breathlessly. It was the most beautiful sound he'd ever heard.

She pressed her hands to either side of his face. "I'm happy again." Her next laugh was partially a sob. "The world is still burning around us, but I'm happy because I have you back."

"You never lost me, darling. You never will." He knew he was grinning like an idiot, but he couldn't help it. Their love for each other had already passed so many tests. They would leave the room in a few minutes, stronger and better than when they'd walked in.

The sound of East clearing his throat had their

heads spinning toward the door leading to the adjoining conference chamber.

East was standing there, looking as snappy as ever in his navy suit. A comical twist rode his lips. "Man! Never before have I rained so hard on anyone's parade by simply stepping into a room." He moved farther into the room and shut the door behind him.

"Then get out," Seven growled, though he was all too aware it wasn't wise for him and Tiffany to be gone from their regular posts much longer.

"I wish I could, but the HR Department is about to close for the evening, and we still have a few things to discuss. Like our moles, as in plural." East pointed at the conference table. "You're gonna want to have a seat for this."

Seven quickly pulled a chair back from the table, sat, and tugged Tiffany into his lap.

East curled his upper lip at them. "You look disgustingly happy. I can barely stand the sight of you."

With a giggle, Tiffany pulled out the nearest chair and slid over to it. "Just in case someone pops their head in the door," she explained breathlessly.

Seven leaned closer to mutter in her ear, "Like that mattered to you a minute ago."

She blushed, and East threw up his hands. "If you're trying to make me feel single and desperately lonely, it's working." He shot a furtive glance at his watch.

Seven knew it was time to get serious. "How many moles are we talking about?"

"Two, at the moment. Could be more." Hiking a hip on the end of the table, East quickly filled them in on how he'd borrowed Goliath's tracking and scenting skills a few nights ago after Seven had gone to bed. Long story short, he was now working as an asset to the FBI. At their request, he'd tried but failed to get the Doberman to track the scent specimens they'd provided of Marcel and Jamal to the two men who'd been working for the past month with Tiffany in the kitchen.

East had subsequently swiped a few drink glasses when the two chefs weren't paying attention in order to run DNA tests on them. The results had come back. They weren't a match, meaning the men posing as Agent Marcel Craft and Agent Jamal Rivera were imposters. The feds had an investigation underway to track the real agents who were missing.

"Mercy," Tiffany whispered at the conclusion of his report.

Holding East's gaze, Seven reached for her hand. "Give me one good reason why I shouldn't make a run for the border with my wife tonight."

East's grin was one hundred percent cocky cowboy. "Actually, I can give you two reasons. The first one is a culinary arts student from the University of Texas. Her name is Helena Sorens, and she'll be interning with you, Tiffany." He paused dramatically. "As of tomorrow."

"Tomorrow!" She shot an amazed look at Seven before returning her attention to East. "Why am I just now hearing about this?"

Seven chuckled as he squeezed her fingers. "I think this is East's way of saying the FBI is about to embed a real team here to keep an eye on the imposter team."

"Bingo." East made a shooting motion at Seven. Then he grinned at Tiffany. "A few days later, the training center is going to finally scrape up the funds for that admin assistant you've been begging for."

"I have?" She chuckled.

"Privately, of course. You'll get to brag all about your growing influence with the powers-that-be to those knotheads posing as federal agents. You'll hint about a few other wonderful changes in the works and gush about how you couldn't have done it without them. Blah, blah, gag me."

Seven nodded thoughtfully. "Any more ideas about what the Megalodon is planning?" *For me?* He glanced furtively at Tiff, silently begging East not to say anything that would scare her too much.

East tapped his fists together. "Now that you ask, there's been some chatter," he informed them carefully. "Enough to give the feds the impression that she's planning something big." He pursed his lips.

"Right here at the training center. That theory is supported by the fact that her biggest shell corporation, Infinity, has awarded a total of six scholarships to students in this rotation, all of which had a part in sending her son to prison. It is further supported by the fact that she's stacking her team on campus. Uncovering Marcel and Jamal as imposters is only the beginning. There may be more coming. There may be others already on site."

"Speaking of which," Seven raised a finger, "I was hoping you'd take a closer look at my squad mate, Cecilia. She copped a feel on my chest holster earlier today. She's pretty hands on, if you know what I mean."

"I do, unfortunately." Tiffany's voice was seething. "You do *not* want to know how many ways I've been dreaming of frying, boiling, and grilling her sorry little self until every inch of her is as red as her hair."

East gave a bark of laughter. "There are so many things I could say right now, but I won't."

Seven's lips twitched, knowing he'd said more than enough in front of his wife.

"Alright, then. Let me do my thing." East stood, still chuckling.

Seven's heart sank at the realization that his long-hoped-for reunion with Tiffany was coming to an end. It was one thing to kiss and make up. They'd done it all too many times in the past. But this time, they weren't simply going back to playing house together. This time, they held jobs in different cities. This time, their future was much less certain. They were surrounded by enemies, and a dangerous criminal mastermind was working day and night to tighten her net around them.

He also hadn't yet gotten around to telling his wife about East's job offer at his private security firm, but it would have to wait.

A light knock on the conference room door signaled to them that their time was up. From the other side, the clerk announced in a sing-song voice that she was heading home and ready to lock up.

For all Seven knew, this would be the last time he spoke to his wife before the final showdown. On their way to the door, he yanked her against him. "No matter what happens next, I love you. I will always love you." He needed her to believe it.

She reached up to touch his cheek. "I love you, too." With one last tender kiss, she slipped from his embrace and left the room ahead of him.

Though East briefly clapped a hand on Seven's shoulder, he didn't say anything.

"My answer is yes about the job," Seven muttered in a low voice. "If I survive what's coming next, there's no one else I'd rather work with."

CHAPTER 10: FEELING THE STING

TIFFANY

Despite a sleepless night and the fear weighing her down on Seven's behalf, Tiffany pasted on a smile and marched into the kitchen the next morning at five o'clock on the dot. Her white jacket was freshly pressed, her boots slick with a new coat of polish, and her lips gleaming with hot pink lipstick.

Go big or go home! She was convinced that Seven's continued safety directly hinged on her ability to continue playing her current role. Keeping in mind that the imposter chefs saw her as a vengeful divorcee, she made sure her lips were twisted in a pout when Marcel glanced her way.

As usual, he'd started work before her. He was lording over his favorite preparation counter, his dark hands coated with bleached white flour beneath the bright fluorescent lights. This morning, he was kneading dough for dinner rolls. She could smell the yeast in the air. They would serve the rolls at both Sunday brunch and Sunday dinner. From past experience, the training center had come to expect a significant percentage of students to sleep in on their only day off, hence the reduction of Sunday meals from three to two. For the students who wanted more to eat, there was a self-serve snack bar in the foyer outside the auditorium. On Sundays, Tiffany and her team stocked it with fruit, granola bars, and other quick-grab items, including chilled water bottles.

Tipping her nose up for a tentative sniff, she nodded in approval at Marcel as he worked. "It smells like the goodness of home in here, which will do wonders for the students' psyche. It's been a long week for them. They're tired and missing the people they love. They've seen a few classmates crash and burn already. Personally, I wouldn't mind watching one man in particular do a little crashing and a whole lot of burning right now." She'd gotten wind of three resignations so far. "But I digress. What I'm trying to say is that a meal made from scratch is exactly what the training center needs today."

Her phone buzzed with an incoming message. She held it up in the air to scan its contents. It was the FBI's daily report on Seven's activities that she was supposed to forward to the phone number the Megalodon had given her during their last fateful meeting. Despite Tiffany's daily check-ins, the woman had yet to respond to a single one of her messages. It was impossible to tell if that was a good thing or a bad thing.

Returning her phone to her pocket, she glided to the sub-zero refrigerator and pulled out six large watermelons, rowing them up beside the sink for washing. To block out her growing list of fears, she'd spent the last half hour perusing food art pictures online for ideas. She'd finally settled on a simple yet clever set of instructions for making duck-like creatures out of the scooped out rinds, then piling the watermelon wedges back into the rind bowls to form fleshy melon "bodies."

As she hummed and rinsed, Marcel's voice sounded low and husky in her ear. "Revenge looks good on you. So does that pink shade of lipstick."

"Thanks." Dread zinged through her at the realization that a murderer was flirting with her. It made her more anxious than ever for the arrival of her new undercover intern. "Are your dinner rolls rising to the occasion?" Trying to sound light and flirtatious, it was all she could do to keep her voice from shaking.

"Always." He chuckled and stepped away as she did a little more splashing than necessary in the sink. "You're right about the students. This is exactly what they need. It's the perfect last meal." At her startled glance, he continued smoothly, "Before they start the grind all over again on Monday."

Last meal. The grisly words hung in the air between them even after she started slicing watermelon. She tried not to think about all the awful things in history that had happened on Sundays — a day of rest and relaxation when so many people let their guard down. The attack on Pearl Harbor was probably the biggest example. Most Americans had been asleep in their beds when the Japanese fleet had sailed into the harbor with such deadly intent.

Kind of like most of the training center's students and cadre are asleep in their beds right now. Tiffany glanced out the window over the sink and was unable to make out much in the darkness.

A flash of lightning and an ensuing clap of thunder made her squeak.

"Jumpy today, are we?" Marcel walked behind her again for no particular reason.

"It's weird weather out there," she muttered, feeling a little foolish. "There's a strange glow to the sky and..." *Good golly!* She leaned closer to the window. It almost looked like fire in the distance. She squinted as she tried to gauge the location of the glow. Unless she was mistaken, it was roughly in the vicinity of the men's dormitory.

"Fire!" she gasped, spinning around. "I think one of the dorms is on fire."

She discovered Marcel standing close — so close that she jolted again and gave a louder yelp than before. "Marcel!" She pressed a shaking hand to her chest. "I wasn't expecting you to be..." *Right there.*

She finished the sentence inside her head as he craned around her for a better look out the window.

"I think you're right." He abruptly reached for her hand. "Come on. Let's get you some place safe."

"Me?" She tried to tug her hand free, but his fingers tightened over hers like a vise. "I'm more worried about what's going on out there, than in—" She broke off her words as he tugged her across the kitchen to stand in front of the walk-in freezer. Horror filled her mouth as she watched him unlatch the door. "What are you doing?"

His expression was unreadable as he yanked open the door. "Believe it or not, this is my way of keeping you safe." He shoved her inside. Though she put up her best struggle, she was no match for his superior strength.

"Marcel!" she gasped, scanning his features in the desperate hope of finding any humanity left in him. "Please don't do this."

"Don't do what?" His voice was resigned. "Exactly how much have you figured out about what's really going on, Mrs. Tiffany Colburn?"

"What are you talking about?" she babbled, wrapping her arms around her middle as her teeth began to chatter from the radiating coldness.

"Don't play dumb." The look he gave her was icier than the frozen slabs of meat hanging from hooks on either side of her. "It's not near as pretty as the revenge you're salivating about getting on your soon-to-be ex-husband. I know you don't trust me. You never have, but that's about to change. Today is the day I get to hand you everything you want the most."

"Why? Wh-what's going on?" she stammered. Her lips were growing stiff from the cold, but it was nothing compared to the block of ice settling in her heart. There was no way Marcel knew what she really wanted. That he assumed it was revenge only proved how well she'd played her role with him.

"You'll find out soon enough, beautiful. You were a vital part in making this happen, by the way. My boss is very, very happy with the reports you've been sending her. We wouldn't have known half as much about the center's security infrastructure without your help, which is why you're being allowed to wait out the storm in here." He shrugged out of his white jacket and tossed it to her. "Put it on. I'll come back for you when it's over." He turned to go, then spun around with one dark hand outstretched. "Oh, and I'll be needing your phone. We don't need any 911 operators getting wind of what's happening outside too soon."

Her hands were shaking so badly that she could barely close her fingers around the cell phone. She dropped it as she handed it to him. Instead of bending down to pick it up, he ground it beneath his heel. Then he exited the freezer and slammed the door in her face, throwing her into complete blackness.

It took her numb brain several seconds to process what had just happened. She tugged on Marcel's jacket, despising as much as appreciating his body heat that was still clinging to it. Then she reached for the burner phone Seven had given her nearly a week ago.

She mashed the speed dial to his number. Though it rang incessantly, he didn't answer.

"Come on, baby! Pick up!" she pleaded. "Come on! Come on! Come on!"

She dialed East's number next. Though he answered right away, she couldn't understand a word he said. His voice was faint and garbled. It was a bad connection, probably due to the steel walls encasing her current location.

"Freezer!" she screamed into the mouthpiece, hoping against hope that he could hear her voice better than she could hear his. "I'm in the freezer!"

The line went dead.

She dialed him back several times, but he didn't pick up again.

In the effort to ward off hypothermia as long as possible, she started bouncing up and down. She jumped until she was tired, then she settled into stretching on her tiptoes and lowering herself back down again and again. It helped a little, but she grew steadily colder.

Instead of the numbness she expected, a stinging sensation stole over her extremities. *That's just great. I'm going to get a mega case of frost bite first. Then I'm going to die.*

SEVEN COULDN'T HEAR MUCH of anything over the scream of fire alarms in the dorm. Lights flashed on, and his classmates swarmed from their beds like ants. Their faces were frozen in expressions of surprise and horror. Their mouths were open in frantic shouts to each other as they tried to make sense of what was happening.

He joined the human tide of bodies barreling toward the exit and made a sickening discovery. The door to the stairwell had been barred shut, and no amount of ramming bedrails or anything else into it could budge it. The elevator proved equally inoperable.

He and his classmates wrapped sections of bed sheets and t-shirts around their mouths and noses as the smoke in the air grew thicker.

Seven's secure phone vibrated with an incoming call. It was East.

Knowing his friend wouldn't be able to hear a word he said, he texted a brief SOS message. All he could do after that was wait.

And wait.

And wait.

And wait.

He watched helplessly as a classmate toppled over, unconscious. The oxygen in the room was rapidly thinning. He kept his own face to the floor, knowing the cleanest air was down low.

When the wall in front of him started to move, he figured he was hallucinating. When East's face appeared, however, he realized help had arrived. A team of cadre flooded the room behind him, wearing an assortment of firefighter gear and gas masks. They fanned out across the smoky room — guiding, dragging, and carrying his classmates toward an exit he wasn't even aware existed until now.

East reached Seven's side and propped one broad shoulder beneath his arm. Then he half-carried and half-dragged him to what turned out to be a hidden set of stairs.

They were encased in steel and led straight down. The spiral stairs made Seven so dizzy that he was soon close to vomiting. They descended a level below where he and his classmates had been sleeping.

When they finally stopped, Seven perceived that they'd arrived at some sort of safe room. Or storm shelter. *Shoot!* Maybe it was a little bit of both. Like the stairwell, the walls were constructed of steel panels. There was a bench built into the wall that ran the perimeter of the room. Blankets were inter-

mittently stacked along it. Above and below the
bench were shelves crammed with supplies — dry
goods, water bottles, medical kits, flashlights, and a
number of other emergency items.

Seven unwound the smokey strip of linen from
his face, coughing uncontrollably until East tossed
him a water bottle. He drank deeply, allowing the
cool water to soothe his raw throat.

"Tiff?" he choked the moment he could speak
again.

East gravely shook his head. "Both imposter
chefs have been arrested, but they're not talking.
They will, though." His voice was cold and clipped.
"Now that the Feds have located the remains of the
two missing agents, they'll be headed straight for
death row. That is, unless they help us bring down
the Megalodon."

Seven nodded as he dialed the number to Tiff's
burner phone. It rang endlessly. After several more
tries, he gave up. "I need to go after her," he cried in a
scratchy voice. A dozen nightmarish scenarios
flashed through his mind of what might've befallen
her.

"It's too soon." East placed his hands on Seven's
shoulders. "The feds have made five arrests so far,
but none of them are the Megalodon. Until she
makes her appearance..."

Seven shook his hands off, unable to shake the

sense of urgency that Tiff needed him. "She should have called by now. Something's wrong."

East held his gaze. "We have every reason to believe the Megalodon has you marked for extermination," he reminded. "Your life in exchange for the one you took from her."

"I'm still going after Tiff," Seven returned coolly. "Without her, mine wouldn't be worth living."

East hesitated a moment before nodding. "Fine, but I'm going with you."

Seven drew an exasperated breath. "You don't have—"

"We're partners, remember?"

"Technically, I'm still an training center student," Seven reminded, trying to give his friend a way out.

East shrugged. "The partnership I had in mind wasn't built on technicalities. We're either both all in, or we're not. Our roles might be reversed next time, and I'd just as soon not be second-guessing whether you're going to have my back when that happens. So, what's it going to be?"

Seven didn't hesitate to hold out his filthy hand. "I'm in."

"Me, too." East rummaged round the room for a First Aid Kit and a few other supplies. Then he rejoined Seven. "Okay. What's the plan?"

Seven's gaze searched for the exit, though he

didn't immediately find it. "I'm going to need the assistance of my other faithful partner.

East smirked. "I presume we're talking about that mammoth Doberman of yours?"

"Yep."

East moved across the room to tap a lengthy code into a digital wall panel. A steel panel slid open. "This way." He motioned for Seven to follow him.

They moved down a subterranean tunnel and surfaced on the campus grounds a good fifty yards or so from the men's dormitory.

The entire building was enveloped in flames. A fire engine screamed in the distance and grew louder. Then another one.

Seven was aghast at the crassness of the Megalodon's latest move. Attempting to burn him alive with over thirty other guys was extreme, even for her.

Signaling for him to remain silent, East led them in a leap frogging maneuver to the dog kennel. After working together in the Texas Rangers, it took little effort to slide back in to their old routine of trading silent signals. They took turns covering each other's backs with their guns drawn while the next guy moved forward.

Raindrops smattered the ground while the wind gusted around them. An occasional flash of lightning splintered the overcast sky, illuminating the campus grounds. Thunder rumbled faintly like cannon fire on a faraway battlefield.

The wail of approaching emergency vehicles had the dogs howling and wailing pitifully by the time Seven and East reached the kennel.

"Do you have a scent specimen?" East hollered as Seven released the frantic Doberman from his cage.

"Nope." Seven felt strangely gleeful despite his negative answer. The lack of a specimen for Tiffany wouldn't slow them down. He and Goliath had practiced this next routine dozens of times. He gave the dog the signal to find her.

The Doberman's response was immediate. He sprinted for the exit and stood there, barking ferociously and pawing at the door. The moment Seven opened it, Goliath leaped forward. His powerful limbs ate up the distance between the kennel and kitchen facility. He stopped when he reached the side door, barking and pawing madly at it.

Hoping it meant that Tiff was inside the building, safe and sound, Seven tried to twist the doorknob, but found it locked.

"Stand back!" East shouted.

Seven pulled the frantic dog a safe distance away while East shot the lock off.

Yanking open the door, East stood to one side as Goliath flew past him into the dim interior. The dreary light seeping through the windows turned the kitchen cabinetry and appliances into menacing shadows.

Seven had no idea where the light switches were, so he flipped on the small flashlight he always kept on hand and held it flush with the barrel of his gun as he followed the dog. He did a few wide sweeps with the light but saw no movement in the building.

Goliath snuffled along the floor and moved in a jerky line across the room, pausing when he reached a wide silver door.

Seven stared, wondering what was behind it.

"It's a freezer," East muttered at his elbow.

"Tiff!" Seven cried hoarsely, setting the safety on his gun and jamming it into his waistband. He moved around the dog to yank on the silver lever handle. Dragging open the oversized door, he shone his flashlight inside.

The beam of light swept across the form of a woman. It was Tiff! She was wrapped in an over-sized white jacket that resembled a shroud. Swaying in his direction, she mumbled something through blue lips.

He lunged for her, lifting her in his arms and cuddling her close to warm her.

Her curvy frame remained limp as he spun with her and exited the icy chamber. She didn't appear capable of speech, so it wasn't immediately clear who had done this to her. Nor did they have any idea when her attacker might return.

"We have to get her out of here!" Seven waffled between heading straight to the storm shelter as opposed to first making a detour to the training center's clinic.

The sound of clapping halted him and East in their tracks.

Cecilia stood in the open doorway of the kitchen, blocking their escape. She'd exchanged her skimpy outfit from dinner to something that resembled a flight suit. It was olive green with the pants legs tucked into her boots. Flipping on a switch as she crossed the threshold, the room was suddenly drenched in light.

She chuckled softly as she advanced on the two men and their precious burden. Goliath hunkered lower, growling at her.

She whipped out a pistol and fired it at the dog. He flattened against the ground with a yelp of pain.

"Stay!" Seven growled at him, unsure how badly he was hurt but knowing the dog was no match for another bullet.

Goliath squealed in the back of his throat, but otherwise remained motionless.

"Well?" The red-headed woman shrugged as she waved her pistol between East and Seven. "We put on a good show, didn't we? The five-star chefs, the redheaded classmate, the fire in the dormitory..."

Redheaded classmate? Seven wasn't surprised to learn that Cecilia was another one of the Mega-lodon's goons, no doubt planted at the training center to shadow his every move. He'd been expecting

East's peek into her background to arrive at the same conclusion.

When Cecilia reached up to yank off her long red hair, however, he had to revise his theory. She wasn't a redhead, after all. It was a wig. She peeled off a Hollywood-grade mask next, and he found himself staring into the features of someone he'd not expected to ever lay eyes on in person. She was high on the nation's most wanted list, a woman who'd always worked from the shadows before now.

The Megalodon hadn't simply placed her cronies undercover at the training center. She'd gone undercover herself. She was standing before him now, ready to commence the final play of her deadly game.

Seven felt sick at the realization that the real Cecilia was probably no longer alive.

The Megalodon tossed aside her mask. "I've enjoyed the hunt," she noted in a flat, unemotional voice. "You're clever, Officer Colburn. Intense. Unpredictable, even." She gestured with her gun again. "Except when it comes to your wife. It didn't matter how far I drove the wedge in your gasping, flailing marriage, I knew you would still come for her. In the end, love was your weakness, as it was mine."

Her smile grew colder as she took another step toward him. "After you took the one person I loved the most from me, I decided to return the favor and take what you love the most." She abruptly trained her pistol on Tiff.

With a snarl of rage, East leaped in front of them.

The Megalodon's gun fired a second time, and East fell to his knees, clutching his chest. With a choking sound, he toppled to his side.

Seven watched him out of the corner of his eye, wanting to run to him but knowing he couldn't. Unless he was mistaken, East's hand was slowly moving along the floor, still gripping his gun. It could only mean one thing. He was wearing a bullet-proof vest, which meant he was still in the game.

Knowing he needed to buy his friend a little time to recover, Seven clutched his wife tighter. The second time the Megalodon had fired her weapon, he'd instinctively swiveled sideways, shielding Tiff as best as he could with his shoulders.

She was starting to twitch and wiggle some in his arms, as if finally discerning the danger they were in.

"You'll have to go through me first," he snarled, figuring that wasn't what the Megalodon was planning. To inflict the maximum amount of pain and suffering on him, she wanted to take out Tiff first. She wanted to make him watch.

"You're not calling the shots anymore, Officer Colburn." The Megalodon stepped abruptly sideways to get a better angle on Tiffany.

As Seven swiveled with his wife again, he felt

her hand move jerkily between them, fumbling with one of the buttons on his shirt.

Well, I'll be! Cautious hope flooded him as her hand moved beneath the plaid fabric and found the holster where his spare gun was strapped. *That's right, darling.* Even while half frozen, she'd not forgotten she was the wife of a Texas Ranger. He felt her draw the weapon from its holster.

"Then again, if you prefer to do things the hard way," the woman in the flight suit muttered, tightening her finger on the trigger.

"Wait!" Seven shouted.

She paused.

It was the only opportunity Tiff needed. She lifted the pistol drunkenly, using Seven's shoulder as leverage as she fired.

The Megalodon's eyes grew round as red seeped through the fabric covering her shoulder — not the one connected to the hand holding her gun, unfortunately. "You sly little fox." Her smile was ugly as she raised her pistol higher and took aim.

Seven abruptly dropped to his knees as she pulled the trigger. The gun in her hand kicked, and the bullet pinged off something metallic behind him.

Before she could fire again, East rolled in her direction and shot the gun from her hand. He capped her knee next, immobilizing her.

Dropping to the floor, she screamed, "You took everything from me!" There was a maniacal light in her eyes as she continued to spew her hatred on Seven.

Uniformed agents descended on the scene. One of them pressed the Megalodon to her belly, cuffing her wrists behind her back.

"Arla Bergström, you are under arrest for seven counts of first-degree murder, blackmail, wire fraud, and conspiracy to murder a federal police officer. You have the right to remain silent..."

After the agents led her away, paramedics hurried into the kitchen. They were rolling two stretchers between them. Seven tenderly laid his wife on the first one, relieving her of the pistol she was still clutching. East staggered to his feet, refusing to lie down on the second one.

"It was just a scratch," he wheezed, gingerly fingering the hole in his shirt left by the bullet.

Seven hastily instructed the paramedics to place Goliath on the spare bed. "He took a bullet for us." Since it was a search and rescue training center, they didn't bat an eyelash about tending to the animal's injury.

"It's over, Seven," Tiffany quavered, reaching blindly for his hand.

"Yeah, darling. It is." He lifted her cold fingers and pressed them to his lips. "They locked her in the freezer," he explained to the medical crew as they rolled her from the room.

Nodding, one of the paramedics ran ahead to the

ambulance outside and returned with a stack of heated blankets.

Tiffany's grateful sigh as they tucked them around her was music to Seven's soul. She was going to be alright.

EPILOGUE

Twelve months later

Seven drove his new company vehicle, a shiny red dual-cab Ford truck, up the freshly paved driveway leading to his grandfather's farm. Well, technically, he was one of the owners now. Skip Colburn had insisted on adding the name of his last living relative to the deed shortly after Seven returned to town. His harrowing stint at the search and rescue training facility was little more than a bad memory, albeit one that was interlaced with a few high moments.

To Seven's everlasting joy and gratitude, Tiff had turned in her resignation and come home with him to Houston.

A flicker of movement on the front porch alerted him to the fact that she'd been anxiously awaiting his arrival from work. She had several big reasons.

Number one, she continued to fret about his safety every time they were apart, because that's just the kind of woman she was. Number two, she owned and operated a wildly popular online cooking show these days. It was impossible for her to film her daily episode until he returned home each evening to help her out with reason number three.

Seven abruptly braked in the circle drive and leaped down from his truck. Slamming the door shut, he jogged around to where Tiff was sitting on the porch steps. Their infant son was nestled in her arms.

He'd jokingly suggested they name him Seven Squared or Eight, but his bride had swiftly vetoed both ideas. Instead, they'd named him Brandon after her father, Bran for short. She stood as Seven approached and held out their son to him.

She was wearing a fitted white chef's coat with a V-neck that perfectly displayed the diamond necklace he'd gifted her for their two-year anniversary last week. It was a perfect match to her diamond and white gold wedding ring that he'd retrieved from the pawn shop a year ago. Hugging the rest of her curves was a long, flowy black skirt. The wind whipped the hem away from her ankles, revealing a sassy pair of wedge heel sandals. Her blonde hair was longer than ever, blowing like silk strands around her face and arms and falling nearly to her waist.

Seven accepted the warm, squirming bundle

from her and cuddled the babe against his chest with one arm. His other hand snaked out to stop his wife as she started to spin away. "Aren't you forgetting something, darling?"

Joining her on the top stair, he cupped the back of her head, fusing their mouths together. This was the highlight of his day every day. Coming home. Being a husband and father. Holding his son. Kissing his wife. It never got old.

She sighed dreamily against his lips. "I love you, Seven."

He kissed her again. "I love you more."

"I seriously doubt it, but if we stand here and argue about it all evening, I'll never get my episode filmed. Oh, and your grandfather will never get a slice of the apple pie I popped into the oven a few minutes ago." She made a comical face at him. "Which would be a catastrophe of epic proportions."

Seven's mouth started to water, just thinking about the pie. Without asking, he knew she'd baked it from the tart little apples she'd picked from Pops' dwarf apple trees out back. His grandfather had been experimenting with them for years in his greenhouse and had finally come up with what he insisted was the perfect hybrid.

As if on cue, the elderly fella clomped his way around the corner of the wrap-around porch. "You heard the woman," he barked at his grandson. "Quit slobbering on her and let her do what she's gotta do to make that pie."

Goliath was trotting at his side. The same day Seven had moved his family out to the farm, he'd retired the dog from search and rescue operations. Though fully recovered from his bullet wound, he was now filling another important role — that of a service dog to Pops, who couldn't see as well as he used to.

Seven snorted out a chuckle as he bent down to scratch Goliath behind the ears, knowing his grandfather had very little understanding of the technical requirements for filming an online cooking show. He glanced over his shoulder at his wife to kiss her with his eyes as she made her escape.

Tiff had already made his grandfather's pie. It was the easiest part of her evening. The hard part would be the next hour or so that she'd spend juggling the remote controls to her array of video cameras while she recited the lines she'd memorized, filming and refilming each segment of tonight's show until it met her expectations. The miracle of it all was that she somehow managed to make their dinner throughout this painstaking process. At the crack of six, she would set her magical culinary creations in the dumb waiter and send them to the first floor dining room. Only after their family dinner did she return to her soundproof studio in the basement to edit all the video segments she'd filmed earlier. Then she'd fuse them together into another one of her award-winning episodes.

He and Pops always referred to the basement as her studio, but it was actually a full-service kitchen now, complete with commercial grade appliances on one end and television equipment on the other. Seven had specially commissioned it with a top builder in the area, then paid cash to have his wife's dream kitchen made into a reality. It had taken nearly every paycheck of his for the past year to make it happen, but Tiff was worth it.

Fortunately, his new job paid well. East Whitlock hadn't been kidding about making him a full partner. They'd even worked out an agreement for him to earn his share of the infrastructure that East already had in place. So far, the newly renamed Whitlock & Colburn Security firm owned a modest-sized home office building on the outskirts of Houston, two armored vehicles, and a small but growing armory of weapons and other gear. They were toying with the idea of hiring a full-time office manager soon to juggle their client appointments, client contracts, and financial spreadsheets.

"Gimme that boy!" Pops sank into the rocker he kept on the front porch, laid aside his cane, and reached for his great-grandson.

Nuzzling the top of Bran's soft head, Seven dragged in a nose full of his milky, powdery smell before handing him over. "Easy," he muttered, not wanting to wake him. Tiff had just finished nursing him. It would be easier on everyone if he slept through the first part of her cooking and filming.

The air was soon filled with the intoxicating scent of pot roast, herbed vegetables, and fresh-baked honey wheat bread.

Seven's stomach growled first. Pops' stomach joined in the mournful course a few seconds later, making them chuckle.

Seven leaned back against the porch railing, folding his arms as he surveyed his family with pride. "We have a hard life," he joked.

"Yep, and yours is about to get a lot harder." Skip Colburn angled his head at something beyond Seven's shoulder.

"Let me guess," Seven muttered. "My mother-in-law has arrived." Tiff had sent him a warning text earlier that Ros would be joining them for dinner this evening.

"What? You got eyes in the back of your head now?" his grandfather chortled as he rocked.

"Please don't say that around Ros," Seven pleaded. "She already thinks I'm the devil incarnate. Heaven only knows what else her superstitious mind might read into a comment like that."

"Is that so?" His grandfather's silvery brows drew together thoughtfully. "Maybe it's time I had a word—"

"No, Pops. It's not time for that." It was never

going to be time for that. Seven was interested in one thing only — keeping the peace. Though Ros was quirky, she and her daughter enjoyed a very close mother-daughter relationship, and he had no plans to put any wrinkles in it.

"Are you kidding?" His grandfather howled, half-rising from his rocking chair.

The movement and sound jostled Bran awake. Seven dove for the whimpering lad, then turned to see what had his grandfather all hot and bothered.

He grimaced at the sight of Ros's front right car tire. It was half rolled on top of one of Pops' prize rose bushes.

"I'm about to show that infernal woman something far worse than the bad luck she's so afraid of," the older gentleman snarled, reaching for his cane. "When I finish with her..."

Before the full wrath of Skip Colburn erupted, Seven jogged down the stairs, gently patting the back of his fussing son.

Ros stepped from her car and held her arms wide. "Oh, you precious, precious boy!" Her hopelessly adoring gaze fastened on her grandchild.

Seven couldn't help thinking that the wide sleeves of her filmy tunic made her look like a royal blue bird about to fly off, but he knew he couldn't be so lucky. Ros was here to spend the evening. Ever since Bran had made his appearance in the world, her visits had been getting longer and more frequent.

"Thanks, Ros. I knew you loved me," he quipped, swooping in to surprise both of them by planting a kiss on her cheek. Desperate times called for desperate measures.

"Oh, for crying out loud!" she snapped. However, a stunned expression rode her round features as she raised her fingers to the spot where his whiskery chin had accidentally scraped.

"Here." Seven placed her grandson in her arms before she had the chance to recover her usual vinegary aplomb. "I think we both know you were referring to Bran and not me." During the exchange, he neatly swiped her car keys from her. "Go," he urged in a teasing voice. "Pops has waited all afternoon to find a new victim to crab to about his arthritis." It was true. His grandfather dearly loved to share scathing anecdotes about the disease crippling his joints.

He hopped inside his mother-in-law's car and drove it forward a few feet to safer ground. Then he hunkered down beside his grandfather's rose bush to pat it back into place. Other than a broken branch and a few crushed blooms on one side, it had survived the attack from Ros's tire.

He jogged back up the porch steps just in time to hear his grandfather drone in a deceptively silky voice, "I know you love looking for patterns in numbers, Ros. Did you know that the number seven is mentioned over six hundred times in the Bible?"

"Now, Skip!" Ros made a scoffing noise as she bent her head to place a noisy kiss on Bran's ear. The babe gurgled with happiness and flailed his tiny fists at her. "I was just commenting on how many days we've gone without rain this month. I wasn't trying to start an argument with your crotchety old self."

"Crotchety!" His silver beard shivered in indignation.

"Hey!" Seven stepped between them. "I don't know about you, but my mouth is already watering just thinking about that apple pie Tiff has in the oven."

"Ooo!" Ros suddenly looked hungry.

"Don't try to change the subject." Skip Colburn clomped his way around his grandson, pounding his cane into the porch floor with each step. "It's past time for Ros to hear this." He stopped in front of her, blocking her path to the porch swing where she'd been headed. Jutting his chin at her, he continued, "God rested from his creation on the seventh day. Jacob worked for seven years to win Rachel's hand in marriage. Naaman, the leper, dipped his diseased body in the Jordan River seven times to get his healing."

"And Seven just happens to be the name of the man who's perfect for me."

Their heads swung toward the front door as Tiffany's voice rang out.

"Tiff!" Seven moved swiftly to stand in front of

her. "What about your show, darling?" He held out his arms as she stepped from the house.

"This is more important." She wrapped her arms around his middle and stood on her tiptoes to explain in a whisper. "Mom texted me to let me know she was here. I figured you could use my help running interference."

"I can handle this," he assured, clasping her shoulders and dipping his head to gaze into her anxious features. "Trust me." He knew how important her work was to her.

"I do trust you, Seven, with my heart and my life." She brushed her lips against his before lowering herself from her tiptoes. "My mother, on the other hand, is in a category of her own."

She blushed when she realized her voice had carried across the porch that had grown strangely silent.

"Like a category 7 hurricane," Pops snickered.

"There's no such thing!" Seven growled, giving his grandfather a warning head shake.

Tiffany gripped two handfuls of her husband's shirt as she waited with her breath held for her mother's response.

Ros took her time walking to the porch swing and plopping her ample figure down on it. "I wasn't too happy about the date you chose to marry my daughter, Seven," she finally said as she bent to make googly eyes at her grandson. "I think it'll be hard for anyone here to deny the string of misfortune that followed such a disastrous decision."

Tiffany flinched in Seven's embrace, no doubt remembering their life-and-death adventure at the search and rescue training center.

"However," Ros continued, smiling beauteously down at the angel in her arms, "I think it's safe to say that this child has set every wrong in your marriage right." She shook her head, sighing. "You two sure do make beautiful babies."

As Tiffany melted in relief against Seven, he muttered in her ear. "Yes, we do." He knew she was hoping to try again soon for baby number two. She adored their son to pieces, but she was longing for a daughter to round out their numbers.

"About that," she whispered, tipping her head back to gaze up at him. Her blue eyes were misty with joy. "I know it's probably sooner than you wanted, but there's something I've been meaning to tell you."

His war whoop echoed off the porch rafters as he lifted her feet from the floor and swung her around in a full circle. He set her down and sealed his mouth over hers.

I'm going to be a dad all over again. When he finally came up for air, his gaze was blurry and his heart was full.

"Seven." Tiffany gently cupped his face. "I was

just going to let you know it's time to replace the bulb again for my zoom lens."

"What?" He stared at her, utterly stunned. "But you said..." Confusion flooded his gut. He'd been so sure she was about to inform him she had another bun in the oven.

"I'm kidding!" Her laughter pealed merrily around his ears. "You guessed right the first time. I'm pregnant."

He picked her up and spun her around again while she hugged him tightly. "You should have seen the look on your face, though. It was priceless."

"I can't wait to see the look on yours when I get even," he warned in a voice gruff with emotion. "Payday is coming, darling."

"Oh, Seven!" she cried softly, ignoring his threat. "I'm so happy that sometimes I don't know how one heart is supposed to contain it all."

"You don't have to do it alone, Tiff. I've got you." He cuddled her closer, letting her happiness spill over him. Despite having a cranky grandfather and a ridiculously superstitious mother-in-law, he knew he was the luckiest guy in the state of Texas right now.

Like this book? Leave a review now!

Texas Hotline Series

Complete series. Read them all!

The Plus One Rescue
The Secret Baby Rescue
The Bridesmaid Rescue
The Girl Next Door Rescue
The Secret Crush Rescue
The Bachelorette Rescue
The Rebound One Rescue
The Fake Bride Rescue
The Blind Date Rescue
The Maid by Mistake Rescue
The Unlucky Bride Rescue
The Temporary Family Rescue

Much love,
Jo

A cowboy private investigator who doesn't want to spend another Christmas alone. A single mom in a pack of trouble, trying to lie low for the holidays. The snowstorm that blows in a few sizzling possibilities.

Following a chance encounter, East Whitlock hasn't been able to get a certain sassy redhead out of his mind. Though the feisty single mom insists she can take care of herself and her small son, he can't stand the thought of anyone so sweet and lovely being alone for Christmas — in a friend's warehouse, no less. Every instinct in him is shouting that she's in trouble, and he happens to have the right skill set to help her. With no family to spend Christmas with, it's not like he has anything better to do, anyway.

Becky Pershing is preparing to go on the run.

Before she hits the road, however, she manages to catch the attention of a former Texas Ranger working an undercover case. Though he's a perfect gentleman, who makes her feel safer when he's around, she refuses to flirt back. She won't be in town long enough to date him, so why bother?

Until the snowstorm of the century hits, stranding her and her son with the one man in Texas whose kind heart she might not be able to resist.

The Temporary Family Rescue
is available in eBook, paperback, and Kindle Unlimited!

Texas Hotline Series
Complete series. Read them all!
The Plus One Rescue
The Secret Baby Rescue
The Bridesmaid Rescue
The Girl Next Door Rescue
The Secret Crush Rescue
The Bachelorette Rescue
The Rebound One Rescue
The Fake Bride Rescue
The Blind Date Rescue

The Maid by Mistake Rescue
The Unlucky Bride Rescue
The Temporary Family Rescue

Much love,
Jo

NOTE FROM JO

Guess what? There's more going on in the lives of the hunky heroes you meet in my stories.

Because...*drum roll*...I have some Bonus Content for

everyone who signs up for my mailing list. From now on, there will be a special bonus content for each new book I write, just for my subscribers. Also, you'll hear about my next new book as soon as it's out (*plus you get a free book in the meantime*). Woohoo!

As always, thank you for reading and loving my books!

JOIN CUPPA JO READERS!

If you're on Facebook, please join my group, Cuppa Jo Readers. Don't miss out on the giveaways + all the sweet and swoony cowboys!

https://www.facebook.com/groups/
CuppaJoReaders

SNEAK PREVIEW: ACCIDENTAL HERO

MATT

I can't believe I fell for her lies!

Feeling like the world's biggest fool, Matt Romero gripped the steering wheel of his white Ford F-150. He was cruising up the sunny interstate toward Amarillo, where he had an interview in the morning; but he was arriving a day early to get the lay of the land. Well, that was partly true, anyway. The real reason he couldn't leave Sweetwater, Texas fast enough was because *she* lived there.

It was one thing to be blinded by love. It was another thing entirely to fall for the stupidest line in a cheater's handbook.

Cat sitting. I actually allowed her to talk me into cat sitting! Or house sitting, which was what it actually amounted to by the time he'd collected his fiancée's mail and carried her latest batch of Amazon deliveries inside. All of that was in addition to feeding and watering her cat and scooping out the litter box.

It wasn't that he minded doing a favor now and then for the woman he planned to spend the rest of his life with. What he minded was that she wasn't in New York City doing her latest modeling gig, like she'd claimed. *Nope.* Nowhere near the Big Apple. She'd been shacked up with another guy. In town. Less than ten miles away from where he'd been cat sitting.

To make matters worse, she'd recently talked Matt into leaving the Army — for her. Or *them*, she'd insisted. A bittersweet decision he'd gladly made, so they could spend more quality time together as a couple. So he could give her the attention she wanted and deserved. So they could have a real marriage when the time came.

Unfortunately, by the time he'd finished serving his last few months of duty as an Army Ranger, she'd already found another guy and moved on. She hadn't even had the decency to tell him! If it wasn't for her own cat blowing her cover, heaven only knew when he would've found out about her unfaithfulness. Two days before their wedding, however, on that fateful cat sitting mission, Sugarball had knocked their first-date picture off the coffee table, broken the glass, and revealed the condemning snapshot his bride-to-be had hidden beneath the top photo. One of her and her newest boyfriend.

And now I'm single, jobless, and mad as a—

The scream of sirens jolted Matt back to the present. A glance in his rearview mirror confirmed his suspicions. He was getting pulled over. *For what?* A scowl down at his speedometer revealed he was cruising at no less than 95 mph. *Whoa!* It was a good twenty miles over the posted speed limit. *Okay, this is bad.* He'd be lucky if he didn't lose his license over this — his fault entirely for driving distracted without his cruise control on. *My day just keeps getting better.*

Slowing and pulling his truck to the shoulder, he coasted to a stop and waited. And waited. And waited some more. A peek at his side mirror showed the cop was still sitting in his car and talking on his phone. *Give me a break.*

To ease the ache between his temples, Matt reached for the red cooler he'd propped on the passenger seat and dragged out a can of soda. He popped the tab and tipped it up to chug down a much-needed shot of caffeine. He hadn't slept much the last couple of nights. Sleeping in a hotel bed wasn't all that restful. Nor was staying in a hotel in the same town where his ex lived. His very public figure of an ex, whose super-model figure appeared in all too many commercials, posters, magazine articles, and online gossip rags.

Movement in his rearview mirror caught his attention. He watched as the police officer finally opened his door, unfolded his large frame from the front seat of his black SUV, and stood. But he continued talking on his phone. *Are you kidding me?* Matt swallowed a dry chuckle and took another swig of his soda. It was a good thing he'd hit the road the day before his interview at the Pantex nuclear plant. The way things were going, it might take the rest of the day to collect his speeding ticket.

By his best estimate, he'd reached the outskirts of Amarillo, maybe twenty or thirty miles out from his final destination. He'd already passed the exit signs for Hereford. Or the beef capital of the world, as the small farm town was often called.

He reached across the dashboard to open his glove compartment and fish out his registration card and proof of insurance. There was going to be no talking his way out of this one, unless the officer happened to have a soft spot for soldiers. He seriously doubted any guy in blue worth his spit would have much sympathy for someone going twenty miles over the speed limit, though.

Digging for his wallet, he pulled out his driver's license. Out of sheer habit, he reached inside the slot where he normally kept his military ID and found it empty. *Right.* He no longer possessed one, which left him with an oddly empty feeling.

He took another gulp of soda and watched as the officer finally pocketed his cell phone. *Okay, then. Time to get this party started.* Matt chunked his soda can in the nearest cup holder and stuck his driver's license, truck registration, and insurance card between two fingers. Hitting an automatic button on the door, he lowered his window a few inches and waited.

The guy heading his way wore the uniform of a Texas state trooper — blue tie, tan Stetson pulled low over his eyes, and a bit of a swagger as he strode to stand beside Matt's window.

"License and registration, soldier."

Guess I didn't need my military ID, after all, to prove I'm a soldier. An ex soldier, that is. Matt had all but forgotten about the Ranger tab displayed on his license plate. He wordlessly poked the requested items through the window opening.

"Any reason you're in such a hurry this morning?" the officer mused in a curious voice as he glanced over Matt's identification. He was so tall, he had to stoop to peer through the window. Like Matt, he was tan, brown haired, and sporting a goatee. However, the officer was a good several inches taller.

"Nothing worth hearing, officer." *My problem. Not yours. Don't want to talk about it.* Matt squinted through the glaring sun to read the guy's name on his tag. *McCarty*.

"Yeah, well, we have plenty of time to chat, since this is going to be a hefty ticket to write up." Officer McCarty's tone was mildly sympathetic, though it was impossible to read his expression behind his sunglasses. "I clocked you going twenty-two miles over the posted limit, Mr. Romero."

Twenty-two miles? Not good. Not good at all. Matt's jaw tightened, and he could feel the veins in his temples throbbing. Looked like he was going to have to share his story, after all. Maybe, just maybe, the trooper would feel so sorry for him that he'd give him a warning. It was worth a try, anyway. *If nothing else, it'll give you something to snicker about over your next coffee break.*

"Today was supposed to be my wedding day." He spoke through stiff lips, finding a strange sort of relief in confessing that sorry fact to a perfect stranger. Fortunately, they'd never have to see each other again.

"I'm sorry for your loss." Officer McCarty glanced up from Matt's license to give him what felt like a hard stare. Probably trying to gauge if he was telling the truth or not.

Matt glanced away, wanting to set the man's misconception straight but not wishing to witness his pity when he did. "She's still alive," he muttered. "Found somebody else, that's all." He gripped the steering wheel and drummed his thumbs against it. *I'm just the poor sap she lied to and cheated on heaven only knew how many times.*

He was so done with women, as in never again going to put his heart on the chopping block of love. *Better to live a lonely life than to let another person destroy you like that.* She'd taken everything from him that mattered — his pride, his dignity, and his career.

"Ouch!" Officer McCarty sighed. "Well, here comes the tough part about my job. Despite your reasons, you were shooting down the highway like a bat out of Hades, which was putting lives at risk. Yours, included."

"Can't disagree with that." Matt stared straight ahead, past the small spidery nick in his windshield. He'd gotten hit by a rock earlier while passing a semi tractor trailer. It really hadn't been his day. Or his week. Or his year, for that matter. It didn't mean he was going to grovel, though. The guy might as well give him his ticket and be done with it.

A massive dump truck on the oncoming side of the highway abruptly swerved into the narrow, grassy median. It was a few hundred yards or so away, but his front left tire dipped down, *way* down, and the truck pitched heavily to one side.

"Whoa!" Matt shouted, pointing to get Officer McCarty's attention. "That guy's in trouble!"

Two vehicles on their side of the road passed their parked vehicles in quick succession. A rusted blue van pulling a fifth wheel and a shiny red Dodge Ram. New looking.

Matt laid on his horn to warn them, just as the dump truck started to roll. It was like watching a horror movie in slow motion, knowing something bad was about to happen while being helpless to stop it.

The dump truck slammed onto its side and skidded noisily across Matt's lane. The blue van whipped to the right shoulder in a vain attempt to avoid a collision. Matt winced as the van's bumper caught the hood of the skidding dump truck nearly head on, then jack-knifed into the air like a gigantic inchworm.

The driver of the red truck was only a few car lengths behind, jamming so hard on its brakes that it left two dark smoking lines of rubber on the pavement. Seconds later, it careened into the median and flipped on its side. It wasn't immediately clear if the red pickup had collided with any part of the dump truck. However, an ominous swirl of smoke seeped from its hood.

For a split second, Matt and Officer McCarty stared in shock at each other. Then the officer shoved his license and registration back through the opening in the window. "Suddenly got better things to do than give you a ticket." He sprinted for his SUV, leaped inside, and gunned it around Matt with his sirens blaring and lights flashing. He drove a short distance and stopped with his vehicle canted across both lanes, forming a temporary blockade.

Matt might no longer be in the military, but his protect-and-defend instincts kicked in. There was no telling how long it could take the emergency vehicles to arrive, and he didn't like the way the red pick up was smoking. The driver hadn't climbed out of the cab which wasn't a good sign.

Officer McCarty reached the blue van first, probably because it was the closest, and assisted a dazed man from one of the back passenger doors. He led the guy to the side of the road, helped him get seated on a small incline, then jogged back to help the next passenger exit the van. Unfortunately, Officer McCarty was only one man, and this was much bigger than a one-man job.

Following his gut, Matt flung off his emergency brake and gunned his motor up the shoulder, pausing a few car lengths back from the collision. Turning off his motor, he leaped from his truck and jogged across the double lane to the red pickup. The motor was still running, and the smoke was rising more thickly now.

Holy snap! Whoever was in there needed to get out immediately before it caught fire or exploded. Arriving at the suspended tailgate of the doomed truck, he took a flying leap and nimbly scaled the cab to reach the driver's door. Unsurprisingly, it was locked.

Pounding on the window, Matt shouted at the driver. "You okay in there?"

There was no answer and no movement. Peering closer, he could make out the still form of a woman. Blonde, pale, and curled to one side. The only thing holding her in place was the snarl of a seatbelt around her waist. A trickle of red ran across one cheek.

Matt's survival training kicked in. Crouching over the side of the truck, he quickly assessed the damage to the windshield and decided it wasn't enough to make it the best entry point. *Too bad.* Because his only other option was to shower the driver with glass. *Sorry, lady!* Swinging a leg, he jabbed the back edge of his boot heel into the edge of the glass, nearest the lock. His luck held when he managed to pop a fist-sized hole instead of shattering the entire pane.

Reaching inside, he unlocked the door and pulled it open. The next part was a little trickier, since he had to reach down, *way* down, to unbuckle the woman and catch her weight before she fell. It would've been easier is she was conscious and able to follow instructions. Instead, he was going to have to rely on his many years of physical training.

I can do this. I have to do this. An ominous hiss of steam and smoke from beneath the front hood stiffened his resolve and made him move faster.

"Come on, lady," Matt muttered, releasing her seatbelt and catching her. With a grunt of exertion, he hefted her free of the mangled cab. Then he half-slid, half hopped to the ground with her in his arms and took off at a jog.

Clad in jeans, boots, and a pink and white plaid

shirt, she was lighter than he'd been expecting. Her upper arm, that his left hand was cupped around, felt desperately thin despite her baggy shirt. It was as if she'd recently been ill and lost a lot of weight. One long, strawberry blonde braid dangled over her shoulder, and a sprinkle of freckles stood out in stark relief against her pale cheeks.

He hoped like heck she hadn't hit her head too hard on impact. Visions of various traumatic brain injuries and their various complications swarmed through his mind, along with the possibility he'd just moved a woman with a broken neck. *Please don't be broken.*

Since the road was barricaded, he carried the woman to the far right shoulder and up a grassy knoll where Officer McCarty was depositing the other injured victims. A dry wind gusted, sending a layer of fine-grain dust in their direction, along with one prickly, rolling tumbleweed. About twenty yards away was a rocky canyon wall that went straight up, underscoring the fact that there really hadn't been any way for the hapless van and pickup drivers to avoid the collision. They'd literally been trapped between the canyon and oncoming traffic.

An explosion ricocheted through the air. Matt's back was turned to the mangled pile of vehicles, but the blast shook the ground beneath him. On pure instinct, he dove for the grass, using his body as a shield over the woman in his arms. He used one hand to cradle her head against his chest and his other to break their fall as best as he could.

A few people cried out in fear, as smoke billowed around them, blanketing the scene. For the next few minutes, it was difficult to see much, and the wave of ensuing heat had a suffocating feel to it. The woman beneath Matt remained motionless, though he was pretty sure she mumbled something a few times. He crouched over her, keeping her head cradled beneath his hand. A quick exam determined she was breathing normally, but she was still unconscious. He debated what to do next.

The howl of a fire engine sounded in the distance. His shoulders slumped in relief. Help had finally arrived. More sirens blared, and the area was soon crawling with fire engines, ambulances, and paramedics with stretchers. One walked deter-minedly in his direction through the dissipating smoke.

"What's your name, sir?" the EMT worker inquired in calm, even tones. Her chin-length dark hair was blowing nearly sideways in the wind. She shook her head to knock it away, revealing a pair of snapping dark eyes that were full of concern.

"I'm Sergeant Matt Romero," he informed her out of sheer habit. *Well, maybe no longer the sergeant part.* "I'm fine. This woman is not. I don't know her name. She was unconscious when I pulled her from her truck."

As the curvy EMT stepped closer, Matt could read her name tag. *Corrigan.* "I'm Star Corrigan, and I'll do whatever I can to help." Her forehead wrinkled in alarm as she caught sight of the injured woman's face. "Omigosh! Bree?" Tossing her red medical bag on the ground, she slid to her knees beside them. "Oh, Bree, honey!" she sighed, reaching for her pulse.

"I-I..." The woman stirred. Her lashes fluttered a few times against her cheeks. Then they snapped open, revealing two pools of the deepest blue Matt had ever seen. They held a very glazed-over look in them as they latched onto his face. "Don't go," she pleaded with a hitch to her voice that might've been due to emotion or the amount of smoke she'd inhaled.

Either way, it tugged at every one of his heartstrings. There was a lost ring to her voice, along with an air of distinct vulnerability, that made him want to take her in his arms again and cuddle her close.

"I won't," he promised huskily, hardly knowing what he was saying. He probably would have said anything to make the desperate look in her eyes go away.

"I'm not loving her heart rate." Star produced a penlight and flipped it on. Shining it in one of her friend's eyes, then the other, she cried urgently, "Bree? It's me, Star Corrigan. Can you tell me what happened, hon?"

A shiver worked its way through Bree's too-thin frame. "Don't go," she whispered again to Matt, before her eyelids fluttered closed. Another shiver worked its way through her, despite the fact she was no longer conscious.

"She's going into shock." Star glanced worriedly over her shoulder. "Need a stretcher over here!" she called sharply. One was swiftly rolled their way.

Matt helped her lift and deposit their precious burden aboard.

"Can you make it to the hospital?" Star asked as he helped push the stretcher toward the nearest ambulance. "Bree seemed pretty intent on having you stay with her."

Matt's brows shot up in surprise. "Uh, sure." As far as he could tell, he'd never laid eyes on the injured woman before today. More than likely she'd mistaken him for someone else. He didn't mind helping out, though. *Who knows?* Maybe he could give her medical team some information about the rescue that they might find useful in her treatment.

Or maybe he was just drawn to the fragile-looking Bree for reasons he couldn't explain. What-ever the case, he found he wasn't in a terrible hurry to bug out of there. He had plenty of extra time built into his schedule before his interview tomorrow. The only real task he had left for the day was finding a hotel room once he reached Amarillo.

"I just need to let Officer McCarty know I'm

leaving." Matt shook his head sheepishly. "I kinda hate to admit this, but he had me pulled over for speeding when this all went down." He waved a hand at the carnage around them. It was a dismal sight of twisted, blackened metal and scorched pavement. All three vehicles were totaled.

Star snickered, then seemed to catch herself. "Sorry. Inappropriate laughter. Very inappropriate laughter."

He shrugged, not in the least offended. A lot of people laughed when they were nervous or upset, which she clearly was about her unconscious friend. "Guess it was pretty stupid of me to be driving these long empty stretches without my cruise control on." Especially with the way he'd been seething and brooding nearly non-stop for the past seventy-two hours.

Star shot him a sympathetic look. "Believe me, I'm not judging. Far from it." She reached out to pat Officer McCarty's arm as they passed him with the stretcher. "The only reason a bunch of us in Hereford don't have a lot more points on our licenses, is because we grew up with this sweet guy."

"Aw, shoot! Is that Bree?" Officer McCarty groaned. He pulled his sunglasses down to take a closer look over the top of them. His stoic expression was gone. In its place was one etched with worry. The personal kind. Like Star, he knew the victim.

"Yeah." Star's pink glossy lips twisted. "She and her brother can't catch a break, can they?"

Since they were only a few feet from the back of an ambulance and since two more paramedics converged on them to help lift the stretcher, Matt peeled away to face the trooper who'd pulled him over.

"Any issues with me following them to the hospital, officer? Star asked if I would." Unfortunately, it would give the guy more time and opportunity to ticket Matt, but that couldn't be helped.

"Emmitt," Officer McCarty corrected. "Just call me Emmitt, alright? I think you more than worked off your ticket back there."

"Thanks, man. Really appreciate it." Matt held out a hand, relieved to hear he'd be keeping his license.

They soberly shook hands, eyeing each other.

"You need me to come by the PD to file a witness report or anything before I boogie out of town?"

"Nah. Just give me a call, and we'll take care of it over the phone." Emmitt pulled out his wallet and produced a business card. "Not sure if we'll need your story, since I saw how it went down, but we should probably still cross every T."

"Roger that." Matt stuffed the card in the back pocket of his jeans.

"Where are you headed, anyway?"

"Amarillo. Got an interview at Pantex tomorrow."

"Solid company." Emmitt nodded. "Got several friends who work up there."

Star leaned out from the back of the ambulance. "You coming?" she called to Matt.

He nodded vigorously and jogged toward his truck. Since the ambulance was on the opposite side of the accident, he turned on his blinker, crossed the lanes near Emmitt's SUV, and put his oversized tires to good use traversing the pitchy median. He had to spin his wheels a bit in the center of the median to get his tires to grab the sandy incline leading to the other side of the highway. Once past the accident, he had to re-cross the median to get back en route. It was a good thing he'd upgraded his truck for off-roading purposes.

They continued north and drove the final twenty minutes or so to Amarillo, which boasted a much bigger hospital than any of the smaller surrounding towns. Luckily, Matt was able to grab a decently close parking spot just as another vehicle was leaving. He jogged into the waiting room, dropped Star Corrigan's name a few times, and tried to make it sound like he was a close friend of the patient. A "close friend" who sadly didn't even know her last name.

The receptionist made him wait while she paged Star, who appeared a short time later to escort him back. "She's in Bay 6," she informed him in a strained voice, reaching for his arm and practically dragging him behind the curtain.

If anything, Bree looked even thinner and more fragile than she had outside on the highway. A nurse was bent over her, inserting an I.V.

"She still hasn't woken up. Hasn't even twitched." Star's voice was soft, barely above a whisper. "They're pretty sure she has a concussion. Gonna run the full battery of tests to figure out what's going on for sure."

Matt nodded, not knowing what to say.

The EMT's pager went off. She snatched it up and scowled at it. "Just got another call. It's a busy day out there for motorists." She punched in a reply, then cast him a sideways glance. "Any chance you can stick around until Bree's brother gets here?"

That's when it hit him that this had been her real goal all along — to ensure that her friend wasn't left alone. She'd known she could get called away to the next job at any second.

"No problem." He offered what he hoped was a reassuring smile. Amarillo was his final destination, anyway. "This is where I was headed, actually. Got an interview at Pantex in the morning."

"No kidding! Well, good luck with that," she returned with a curious, searching look. "A lot of my friends moved up this way for jobs after high school."

Emmitt had said the same thing. "Hey, ah..." He

hated detaining her a second longer than necessary, since she was probably heading out to handle another emergency. However, it might not hurt to know a few more details about the unconscious Bree if he was to be left alone with her. "Mind telling me Bree's last name?"

"Anderson. Her bother is Brody. Brody Anderson. They run a ranch about halfway between here and Hereford, so it'll take him a good twenty minutes or so to get here."

"No problem. I can stay. It was nice meeting you, by the way." His gaze landed on Bree's left hand, which was resting limply atop the white blankets on her bed. It was bare of a wedding ring. *Why did I look? I'm a complete idiot for looking.* He forced his gaze back to the EMT. "Sorry about the circumstances, though."

"Me, too." She shot another worried look at her friend and dropped her voice conspiratorially. "Hey, you're really not supposed to be back here since you're not family, but I sorta begged and they sorta agreed to fudge on the rules until Brody gets here." She eyed him worriedly.

"Don't worry." He could tell she hated the necessity of leaving. "I'll stay until he gets here, even if I get booted out to the waiting room with the regular Joes."

"Thanks! Really." She whipped out her cell

phone. "Here's my number in case you need to reach me for anything."

Well, that was certainly a smooth way to work a pickup line into the conversation. Not that Matt was complaining. His sorely depleted ego could use the boost. He dug for his phone. "Ready."

She rattled off her number, and he quickly texted her back so she would have his.

"Take care of her for me, will you, Matt?" she pleaded anxiously.

On second thought, that was real worry in her voice without any trace of a come-on. Maybe Star hadn't been angling for his number, after all. Maybe she was just that desperate to ensure her friend wasn't going to be left alone in the ER. He nodded his agreement and fist-bumped her.

She tapped back, pushed past the curtain, and was gone. The nurse followed, presumably to report Bree's vitals to the ER doctor on duty.

Matt moved to the foot of the hospital bed. "So who do you think I am, Bree?" *Why did you ask me to stay?*

Her long blonde lashes remained resting against her cheeks. It looked like he was going to have to stick around for a while if he wanted answers.

———

I hope you enjoyed the first chapter of

BORN IN TEXAS #1: Accidental Hero.
Available in eBook, paperback, and Kindle Unlimited!

The whole alphabet is coming! Read them all:
A - Accidental Hero
B - Best Friend Hero
C - Celebrity Hero
D - Damaged Hero
E - Enemies to Hero
F - Forbidden Hero
G - Guardian Hero
H - Hunk and Hero
I - Instantly Her Hero
J - Jilted Hero
K - Kissable Hero
L - Long Distance Hero

Much love,
Jo

Heart Lake

The cowboy bad boy who broke her heart years ago and the career opportunity that offers them a second chance at happily-ever-after...

While they were growing up, Hope Remington was the darling of Heart Lake, and Josh Hawling was...well, bad news. And now she's returning after ten years of being gone, with a PhD and plans to use her new position to transform their struggling high school into a center for educational excellence.

She soon realizes that her biggest challenge isn't going to be the rival gangs embedded in the student body, although they're a close second on the list. It's Josh Hawling, who has somehow convinced their aging superintendent that he and his security firm partner can coach their backwoods collection of farm boys into a football team that'll make the playoffs.

How is a woman of her refined background and education supposed to improve test scores and gradu-ation rates when her students' biggest idol is a man who spent more time in the principal's office than in the classroom? Even though she feels safer having him on their crime-ridden campus, she's so not looking forward to her daily encounters with his cocky self. Or being socked in the heart all over again by his devastating smile. Or having to finally face her unwanted attraction that might have kindled into a lot more if she'd never left Texas in the first place.

Welcome to Heart Lake! A small town teaming with old family rivalries, the rumble of horses' hooves, and folks on both sides of the law and everywhere in between — faith-filled romance that you'll never forget.

Winds of Change

Available in eBook, paperback, hard cover, and Kindle Unlimited!

Read them all!

Winds of Change
Song of Nightingales
Perils of Starlight
Return of Miracles
Thousands of Gifts
Race of Champions
Storm of Secrets
Season of Angels

Much love,
Jo

ABOUT JO

Jo is an Amazon bestselling author of sweet and inspirational romance stories about faith, hope, love and family drama with a few Texas-sized detours into comedy. She also writes sweet and inspirational historical romance as Jovie Grace.

1.) Follow on Amazon!
amazon.com/author/jografford

2.) Join Cuppa Jo Readers!
https://www.facebook.com/groups/
CuppaJoReaders

3.) Follow on Bookbub!

https://www.bookbub.com/authors/jo-grafford

4.) Follow on Instagram!
https://www.instagram.com/jografford/

5.) Follow on YouTube
https://www.youtube.com/channel/
UC3R1at97Qso6BXiBIxCjQ5w

amazon.com/authors/jo-grafford

bookbub.com/authors/jo-grafford

facebook.com/jografford

instagram.com/jografford

Made in the USA
Monee, IL
20 February 2023